BEER and GASOLINE

by John Knoerle

This is a work of fiction.

Published by **Blue Steel Press**

Chicago, IL

bluesteelpress@att.net

johnknoerle.com

First edition – first printing, 2017

Cover art and design by Katherine Bennett

ISBN 978-0-6929082-9-7

Library of Congress Number 2017904763

Printed in the United States.

Also by John Knoerle:

"Crystal Meth Cowboys"

"The Violin Player"

The American Spy Trilogy

"A Pure Double Cross"

"A Despicable Profession"

"The Proxy Assassin"

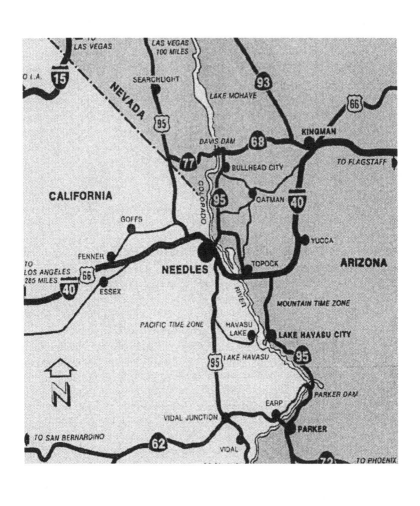

Dear Reader,

This collection of documents is not a book in the traditional sense. Yet it tells an important story. How this collection came to be will be revealed in due course.

In the meantime, please read on.

- ed.

Out here in the Mojave you get asked one question one hell of a lot. How do you handle the damn heat? What yer sposed to say is over a hunnert degrees you cannot tell the difference. But that aint true.

At 110 degrees yer eyeballs swell and it hurts to blink. At 115 yer tongue swells and yer words get slurred. At 120 degrees yer brain locks up and yer mouth hangs open cause it hurts to breathe through yer nose and after about fifteen minutes yer whole body starts to shake. You shiver. You shiver in the heat.

I cannot say what happens over 120 degrees. For an answer to that question you will have to ask one of the old men around here that is more snake than human.

The Mojave holds the record for the hottest temperature ever recorded on earth: 134 degrees, July 10, 1913, Furnace Creek. It is a point of local pride.

Heat is like a member of the family here: raggedy ass young brother, stern mama or drunken uncle, depending. But it is a member of the family, it is here to stay.

I never have lived in a cold climate like the Arctic Circle where spit freezes fore it hits the ground. I read on that. We also have our struggles with the liquid state. There are times in the season when the ground is so hot the rain from a thunderstorm turns to steam fore it touches dirt.

Heat is energy. It pushes back.

You freeze to death it is peaceful like. Like falling to a deep sleep.

You die of heat it is torture.

TRANSCRIPT: Patrol Officer Thomas A. Bell, Needles Police Department

29 May, 1968, 0800-0846 hours. Twenty-nine Palms Marine Corps Air/Ground Combat Center

Building 8-B

INTERROGATING OFFICER:	ROLLTOP
OTHERS ATTENDING:	None
RECORDED:	Y
TRANSCRIPTION BY:	TSJ-23
STATUS:	Level 2, unredacted

ESTABLISHING: Camp Commander Joseph Washburn eschewed local public refuse collection for Camp Harrison, commonly known as Camp X, due to security concerns. CI Chief of Staff dispatched ROLLTOP to the Mojave Desert when Commander Washburn reported that the camp's privately-contracted trash hauler, Jeremiah McLemore, missed two of his thrice-weekly pickups and could not be contacted by telephone.

On Monday, 27 May, ROLLTOP called at McLemore's residence without success. Neighbors reported no recent sightings. That day ROLLTOP also visited the Needles Police Department – the local agency closest to Camp X's location –

and identified himself as Lt. Richard Nolan of the U.S. Army, liaison to Camp X. He circulated a photo of the missing man.

The radio dispatcher and the other patrol officer present did not recognize the man in the photo but officer Thomas A. Bell stated that he knew McLemore from The Rails, a local tavern. When Ofc. Bell inquired what Jeremiah McLemore had to do with Camp X, ROLLTOP told him that McLemore was the Camp's trash hauler, which caused Bell to "turn pale and lose his tongue."

Sensing that Bell was about to reveal sensitive information about Jeremiah McLemore in the presence of the others, ROLLTOP concluded the conversation by inviting Officer Bell out for a beer to "get some background on your friend."

ROLLTOP did not want to excite gossip by meeting at The Rails, but Ofc. Bell said that there were only two bars in town, the other being The Red Dog where, "coppers aren't welcome."

Not wanting to compromise his domicile, ROLLTOP agreed to meet Bell at The Rails that evening. At that meeting ROLLTOP told Bell that McLemore might be in grave danger.

Bell expressed surprise, then said that McLemore told him he had been approached by an out-of-town stranger about his trash collection services, a man offering money to examine the refuse McLemore collected. McLemore told Bell he considered the man "suspicious."

ROLLTOP asked Ofc. Bell if he had shared this information with anyone. Bell stated that he had not. ROLLTOP asked Bell to keep it that way and Bell agreed.

ROLLTOP made arrangements to interview Bell in a more secure setting. Bell agreed to try and determine his friend's whereabouts without opening an NPD missing person's investigation.

INTERVIEW

29 May, 1968

RT: Officer Bell, thank you for making the trip out here to 29 Palms. Here's some gas money.

OB: (opening an envelope) Fifty bucks. Shit, I could drive across the country on fifty bucks.

RT: It's what the DoD calls a travel stipend to pay for your time and trouble.

OB: I've got plenty of time and this weren't no trouble, but thank the Department of Defense for me.

RT: I'll make a note to do that.

OB: Well?

RT: Well, what?

OB: I don't see you writin' it down.

RT: (laughter) I made a mental note. Now, tell me something about your friend Jeremiah McLemore.

OB: Well, he don't say much, which suits me fine. My pals say I'm like an all-night radio station, they can tune in any old time and know there's always something on. So mostly I talked and he listened and laughed at my jokes and bought me beers and, no, he wan't lookin' to take advantage of my tender virtue. He just makes more dough than me – rookie cop on the NPD makes only 300 bucks a month if you can believe that – and Jer had his own business.

Solid citizen and all that but he could knock 'em back with the best of 'em, though I never knew him to slur his words or trip over a chair leg when he left – I'm twenty-one and he's an old man of thirty-eight – so he heads home sooner than me. I would've driven him home if I thought he was deuce.

RT: And you weren't?

OB: Beer's just fuel to me, I got the pulse rate of a jackrabbit. Besides, the desert runs on two things.

RT: Yes?

OB: I'm just settin' up the punch line.

RT: Okay, and what two things does the desert run on?

OB: Beer and gasoline.

RT: That's funny.

OB: And true.

RT: Have you had any success in locating Mr. McLemore?

OB: Negative, Lieutenant···sorry, lost the name.

RT: Nolan.

OB: No luck so far, Lieutenant Nolan. Nobody at The Rails has seen him. He's still got money in the bank but his truck is gone. And him and his truck are the same person.

RT: I saw his truck, it was parked in his driveway.

OB: Good God, that's his hauler, not his truck! His truck is a 1963 Willys Jeep Wagon with a 400 hp, 451 cubic inch Chevy motor and four-wheel drive, hottest truck in San Berdoo County. You don't haul trash in it. Shit, Jer won't even let me use the ashtray.

RT: Okay, got it.

How do we know McLemore didn't jump in his Willys and head up to Vegas to cruise the Strip?

OB: Then he would have had Ramon, his part-timer, do his pickups for him. Jer stiffs his customers, he don't get paid. Jer don't get paid, they repo his truck.

RT: Does McLemore have a lady friend?

OB: Nope. He had a nasty divorce a few years back, she was ballin' his best friend, put him off women, though he'll take a run over to Bullhead City if he needs some tendin' to. 'I'm a renter, not a buyer' is how he puts it.

RT: You check with next-of-kin?

OB: He's got no kids, mom's dead, dad's in a home in Grand Island, Nebraska, where he's from. We left it to you Fan Belt Inspectors to run down his sibs.

RT: I'm not with the FBI, officer.

OB: Yeah, well, there's all kind of federal cops.

RT: That's true.

OB: You gonna toss me a hint here?

RT: No, officer, I am going to let you use that jackrabbit energy to speculate yourself into a coma.

OB: Shit.

RT: So, Jeremiah McLemore, having run a successful commercial trash-hauling service in Needles and the surrounding communities for the better part of six years, has now disappeared for no apparent reason. Is that correct?

OB: Yes sir, though I'm not sure what you mean by apparent.

RT: Apparent. Something that's obvious, something capable of being clearly understood.

OB: Sure. But seems like it also has a slipperyer meaning. Apparent is the same as appearing, right? And what's the first thing you hear when you enter the House of Horrors ride at the county fair?

RT: It's been a while. Remind me.

OB: All things are not as they appear.

RT: During our initial meeting at the police station you looked surprised when I mentioned that McLemore was hauling trash for Camp X.

OB: Jer never said a word about it.

RT: Good, he wasn't supposed to.

OB: But he was gonna tell me Thursday night⋯

RT: Presumably.

OB: Is Jer in trouble?

RT: Well, he was supposed to contact the Camp Commander if he ran into trouble.

You said McLemore told you he had been approached by a stranger earlier in the day, a stranger who expressed interest in examining the trash that McLemore had been collecting. Do I have that right?

OB: That's what he told me.

RT: How did he tell you?

OB: Huh?

RT: In person?

OB: Uh uh. On the phone.

RT: He called you at work?

OB: No sir, Jer's careful-like. He wouldn't take a chance on Cindy listening in.

RT: Your receptionist?

OB: Yes sir.

RT: And what did McLemore tell you on your home phone?

OB: To make sure to stop by The Rails the next night, Thursday, so he could fill me in - it was late on Wednesday and he wanted to crash. Late for him anyway.

RT: What time would that be?

OB: 2200 or so. I could hear Jerry Dunphy in the background. Jer loves the ten o'clock news, not sure why cause he hates Jerry Dunphy.

Anyway, Jer didn't show on Thursday. And then the weekend went by in a purple haze and you showed up on Monday morning.

RT: In our conversation at The Rails you said that McLemore found the stranger who approached him suspicious. Did he say why?

OB: No sir.

RT: Did he tell you the stranger's name.

OB: Yes, because he thought it was odd. Wendell.

RT: Did he characterize Wendell in any particular way? (pause) Take your time.

OB: Well, Jer's a country fair mimic. He taught me how to do an Irish brogue – trick is to whinny your voice like a horse. Don't laugh, it's true.

When Jer told me about Wendell I remember he said, "This one I do not trust."

RT: Was that supposed to be a Russian accent?

OB: It was supposed to be Boris Badenov.

RT: Who is Boris Badenov?

OB: The Russian spy on Rocky and Bullwinkle. A kid's cartoon, very funny.

RT: I'll take your word on that. Did McLemore's use of a Russian accent in characterizing the stranger who approached him about his trash-hauling business lead you to draw any conclusion about the identity of the stranger?

OB: Are you sure you're a lieutenant, Lieutenant, cause you're talkin' just like a lawyer.

RT: I'm not crazy about it myself, officer, but we are on the record here.

OB: Well, I'm not sayin' his Boris Badenov impression led me to any exact conclusion but it sure as shit suggested that this guy was not a local yokel and, seeing as how it's summertime, summertime, sum-sum-summertime in the match head of California, you gotta wonder what would bring someone out here for a visit.

RT: Any theories?

OB: Seems pretty obvious this stranger was interested in your little place across the river there in Arizona.

RT: Yes?

OB: Nobody here is sure what goes on there but one rumor is it's a fed nuke bunker in case of an ICBM attack.

RT: Interesting.

OB: And there's another theory lately.

RT: Let's hear it.

OB: It's an indoctrination compound for future spies who have been smuggled out of orphanages. With no parents, they won't be missed.

RT: That's a good one.

OB: Yeah, there ain't much to do round here. But I think I know what's really going on.

RT: Enlighten me.

OB: Cinder Cones is right up the road.

RT: Yes, I've heard about them. Huge black and red volcanic mounds dating back millions of years.

OB: Just like the moon.

RT: The moon has volcanoes?

OB: Not sure, doesn't matter. Point is Cinder Cones is a moonscape where Apollo astronauts are training in the dark of night for the first-ever lunar landing and Camp X is where they bunk at night.

RT: Nice try, officer, but it's just a training camp.

OB: Could be. I've seen the barracks.

RT: How did you manage that?

OB: I have a pal who runs a helicopter service, we did us a flyover.

You don't look happy.

RT: It's not something we encourage.

OB: Well, you'll need some serious ack ack to back off Clovis. He cut his teeth crop dusting, they fly at twenty feet and duck under the phone lines to save gas on turns.

Then Clovis flew Huey's for a hitch in Nam, and now he's got himself an old Bell bubble chopper held together by duct tape and good intentions but, like Jer and his truck, they are always one and the same.

You need a trusty steed out here.

RT: What's
yours?

OB: '66 Plymouth Belvedere 383 V-8. I call it the
Firechicken.

RT: Cute.

OB: You know, Lieutenant, it's not the barracks you got
out there that's got local tongues to waggin'.

RT: No?

OB: C'mon, you know what I'm talkin' about.

RT: Tell me anyway.

OB: The gray steel building in the middle of the
compound with smoked windows and all kind of antennas
and microwave dishes on the roof.

RT: Noted. Now, I'd like to change the subject.

OB: Sure.

RT: Here's the difficulty. I also do not believe your
friend Jeremiah went to Vegas to cruise the strip. As you
indicated he was very scrupulous about his work schedule
and he missed two trash pickups last week.

OB: Uh huh. Is there something else you're chewin' on?

RT: I know Needles PD doesn't have aerial surveillance
capability and I'd rather not bring the Sheriff's Search and
Rescue Team into this just yet. I prefer local talent

whenever possible. I would like to pay your pal Clovis to do an airborne grid search, say a radius extending five miles outside Needles.

OB: You think Jer is out there in the desert somewhere?

RT: There's one way to find out.

OB: You think he's dead?

RT: That's the logical assumption under the circumstances.

OB: Murdered?

RT: That's what I fear.

OB: Christ. Based on what?

RT: I can't answer that question just now.

OB: This has to do with your goddamn Camp X, doesn't it?

RT: It could, officer, but not necessarily in the way you suspect. Did you know your friend Jeremiah was a Korean War vet?

OB: Sure. He was dishonorably discharged after he went AWOL and was found passed out in a whorehouse in···whatever the capital of South Korea's called.

RT: Seoul. And Jeremiah McLemore was court martialed as a deserter and served 14 months in the brig at Fort Sill, Oklahoma.

OB: Huh, didn't know that. Least it's warm in OK.

RT: What did he tell you about his Korean service?

OB: The thing you need to know about Jer was that he was a born desert rat, hated Nebraska winters. It's why he enlisted, the recruiter told him he'd be stationed in Panama, which he was. Then the war came along and he was sent to the mountains of Korea in the dead of winter. Cold, insanely bone-cutting cold was how he put it. He bailed after three months but he feels bad about it to this day. Or yesterday. Or whatever day it was he was murdered.

RT: We don't know that, officer.

OB: But that's the logical assumption under the circumstances!

I know what you feds are going for here. I swear, sometimes I'm so smart I scare myself.

RT: I often felt that way when I was your age.

OB: Yeah, well···

RT: But I'm happy to hear what you have to say.

OB: Happy?

RT: Yes. Happy.

OB: Well, I've read up on you boys. Everyone in the DoD and the CIA is a conspiracy nut cause they're worried about···what'd they call it?···sedition from within. Everyone is freaking out about sedition from within.

Maybe you didn't know about his court martial when you hired Jer – you know how screwed-up government records are – but then it popped up and you found out he'd marched in some Vets Against the War protests and decided he was a commie pinko lookin' to sell out your super-secret Camp X to the Russians.

Am I comin' through here?

RT: I'm still listening.

OB: Well, now, you're about to turn Jer over to the FBI when – bam – he disappears. You figure a rat inside your operation has tipped him off – it's sedition from within!

So what's Jer's only out? Stage his own murder! Make it look like he was ambushed in his truck while he was out smokin' dope under the night sky while blasting his eight-track like he liked to do – he'd smear some of his blood on the dashboard maybe and let you feds conclude he'd been offed by foreign agents and buried in the desert. That way he could avoid a nationwide dragnet and fly off to Mother Russia.

RT: Where it's very cold.

OB: I'm not sayin' he did that. I'm sayin' that's what you think he did.

RT: Give us some credit for making logical assumptions, officer.

OB: So···You think Jer's truck is out there in the desert and him with it?

RT: Would he leave it behind?

OB: No way.

RT: Which is why I would like to hire your friend Clovis to do a search.

OB: But not San Berdoo Search and Rescue, which is what SOP says we should do next.

RT: You're free to file a police report, officer, but...

OB: We'd have to go through the Sheriff's Office and it'd take a week to get a search together.

RT: That's what I was thinking. (pause) There is one item, Officer Bell, that seems to call your friend's credibility into question.

OB: Yeah?

RT: If McLemore really was approached by a suspicious stranger, what possible reason could that stranger have given him for wanting to paw through piles of refuse which, this time of year, have got to stink to high heaven?

OB: Shit don't stink in the Mojave in the summertime, Lieutenant. It's dust in ten minutes, which is why you need to get yourself a kerchief. And I just read an article in Time magazine that might answer your question.

RT: Pray tell.

OB: Consumer research is a big thing now on Madison Avenue.

RT: That's not exactly news.

OB: But consumer disposal research is the new thing, where they paw through the trash to see what customers are eating or tossin' out.

RT: And why would Madison Avenue research firms be interested in···this part of the world?

OB: You were about to say shithole, weren't ya?

RT: Not at all.

OB: Well, you asked me to answer a hypothetical question, Lieutenant, which I did. What you're asking me now is like putting my hearsay witness on the stand.

RT: Your hearsay witness?

OB: It's a cop joke.

RT: A hearsay witness is some sort of metaphor?

OB: Some sort.

RT: I'm not following.

OB: You are asking me to explain why Jeremiah McLemore didn't reject a stranger's well-paying offer to examine his trash hauls because it was a weird request.

But Jeremiah McLemore did reject the weird request. He called the cops – me!

RT: He called you to set a time to talk about it. And he didn't do it right away.

OB: He called me that night.

RT: A lot can happen in twenty-four hours, officer.

OB: Okay, but I think you need to get yourself a new hearsay witness.

Lieutenant.

RT: I apologize if this is coming across as a hostile interrogation, officer. That is not my intent.

You look surprised.

OB: I've never been apologized to by a lieutenant before.

RT: I guess there's a first time for everything.

Your personnel jacket says you grew up in Florida. How did you come to be a cop in Needles?

OB: My mom lent me money to promote a Country Joe and the Fish concert in Sacramento. We moved there two years ago when she got a job at the State Department of

Agriculture. I went to work as a DJ at a Sacto radio station for shit wages. I partnered up with a buddy to make a quick pile on the concert. Long story short we lost our shirt. Mom said I know how you can pay back the loan. The state is hiring ag inspectors at the Arizona border. So I joined the fruit police.

RT: The who?

OB: California fruit growers were gettin' hit by infestations of the citrus white fly. They said the little buggers were hitchhiking in on fruits and veggies carried by out-of-state visitors.

So I dug through bags of fruit and veggies on Route 66 for six months and got to know the local coppers, did ride along's after shift, helped out. They're spread thin out here. Chief Haney asked me to sign on when he had a vacancy.

RT: You didn't go through academy training?

OB: Hell no. They gave me a written test.

RT: Was it tough?

OB: Hardest part was sharpening the pencil. I couldn't be sworn till I was twenty-one so I spent four months as a jailer and desk officer. My swearing-in ceremony was, 'Here's your badge, here's your gun. Don't fuck it up.'

RT: Interesting. (pause) Officer Bell, I'm curious about something. Is that a sap on your gunbelt?

OB: Yes sir. Sprung steel and lead filings.

RT: Is that legal?

OB: Department issue. They're great for close-in work. With a baton, if you're dancin' with some shithead, you gotta step back to unsheathe the damn thing. Only takes two seconds, but it might be two seconds you don't have.

You said a lot can happen in twenty-four hours, Lieutenant, and that's true. And when you're a copper a lot can happen in two seconds.

RT: Touché, officer.

TRANSCRIPT END

My darling girl,

My third day here and I am already missing you terribly. It is one of the many plagues of this profession that I cannot share with you the details of my undertakings. That's to be expected. But it is monstrous that we cannot share this new thing that I have found — the Mojave Desert.

I flew into 29 Palms Marine Base from Phoenix. We crossed many miles of pinkish sand dotted with towering saguaro cactus; the ones you see in John Wayne movies, their arms raised to the sky. No sign of them here.

Then we crossed stretches of mountainous wasteland in southern Nevada that were the color of chalk, not a speck of life to be seen. Could have been the moon.

But this part of the great Southwest is different. Locals call it the rainshadow desert. There's dew on the ground here if you get up early enough to see it. And the Joshua trees have leaves - ugly, knife-edged things, but leaves.

It is humbling, this ancient seabed with its towering mountains. I am told that, on top of those peaks, one can see the Bull Valley

Mountains in Southern Utah more than two hundred miles away. One fine day we will have to find out if that is true.

I had pictured the desert as dun-colored and so it appears at first. A second look reveals more — slabs of rock varnished a shiny brown, red lichen on outcroppings of lava, dusty green vegetation the locals call scrub.

What the desert landscape doesn't have is blue, save for the vast sky of course. Which gives the vague impression that this enormous expanse of land is still submerged.

This lack of blue escaped me until a helicopter ride took me above an abandoned copper mine with mounds of tailings piled high. Most were a dark green but a few were blue as the Aegean. The blue that makes white violets so beautiful. The blue that makes your white skin and black hair so heart-stopping.

You must see this prehistoric place. With me. The locals are crazy for it.

With tender kisses to you and our beloved Helen, I sign myself,

Your devoted swain

May 25, 1970

To whom it may concern:

As a spy I was forbidden to keep a journal or diary. I did so anyway, for reasons that will become evident.

The following is my account of our search for missing trash collector Jeremiah McLemore on 29 May, 1968. It was compiled from same day notes and my surreptitious recordings of Needles PD Officer Thomas Bell, helicopter pilot Clovis Boudreaux and, later that day, a Paiute Indian nicknamed Billy Chickenplucker.

My mini-cassette recorder was disguised as a soft pack of Winston cigarettes which I carried in my breast pocket. (In the transcript my statements are indicated by my cover ID, Lt. Nolan.)

I typed and transcribed copious notes about the subsequent events in this operation when it became clear to me that it was a potential bombshell. However, I didn't document our search for the remains of Jeremiah McLemore at the time it occurred because I didn't realize its significance. It was not until after my resignation from the CIA that I wrote this account.

With God as my witness: I have no axes to grind or scores to settle. My sole intent is to preserve for posterity a factual record of that particular time and place.

Said record - including personal correspondence and copies of privileged CIA cables - has been kept in a combination safe under my direct supervision. No one else has seen it or knows of its existence.

I destroyed the mini-cassettes pertinent to the unauthorized search because, should they fall into the hands of an eager prosecutor, they might be used as evidence against the boys.

Not right. The scrappy, above-mentioned boys shouldn't pay a price for playing along with my dumb idea.

However, as there are no recordings in evidence, I find myself in the awkward position of being that mythical creature known in police circles as a hearsay witness.

Needles PD Officer Thomas Bell would be amused. To wit:

The morning was clear and dry, temp in the mid 90's at 0900. We met at Clovis Boudreaux's adobe hacienda east of Needles, across the river in Arizona. Clovis' Bell bubble copter was housed in a barn behind his house.

Boudreaux and Jeremiah McLemore were casual friends. Boudreaux had a theory about where JM might have gone. He flew Ofc. Bell and me to a remote spot in the desert about 10 miles north of Needles; a spot where he and JM liked to drink beer and shoot empties with their hunting rifles, doors of the Jeep winged open, music blaring.

Sure enough we spotted the Willys Jeep from the air and landed a short distance away. Bell told Clovis to stay put despite his strenuous objections. Bell and I walked in. What the boys liked about the spot was evident. No roads nearby, no hiking trails; nothing but splendid isolation.

Three feet from the Jeep we found a badly damaged body proned-out, the face twisted to the right, ravaged beyond recognition.

Even the eyes were gone. Bell thought it the work of coyotes. And crows.

The body was approx the right size and height, and Bell ID'ed the clothing as belonging to Jeremiah McLemore.

The driver's door was winged open. The truck ignition was in the on position and the 8-track tape player engaged. The AC was set to max, but of course the truck had run out of gas.

Inside the Willys Jeep we found a fifth of Jose Cuervo that was one-third full, and a half-smoked marijuana cigarette on the eight-track player. On the passenger's side, on the floor, we found an open cooler containing a mix of water and Mountain Dew. Presumably the cooler's ice had melted and the cans of Mountain Dew had exploded in the heat. The cooler was crawling with fire ants, as was the bottle of tequila and much of the cab.

The evidence suggested the following scenario: Jeremiah McLemore, concerned about the suspicious man who had approached him, went to his favorite spot in the desert to calm his nerves, consumed too much alcohol and marijuana and, during the hottest part of the day, stepped out of the truck to urinate. When he did that he hit the wall of heat and collapsed.

Ofc. Bell disagreed w. my scenario.

Bell: "I never knew Jer to drink Mountain Dew with tequila."

Bell seated himself in the driver's seat after swatting out the fire ants. I realized we were contaminating a possible crime scene but that was Bell's concern not mine. My job was to gather as much intel as possible before other agencies got involved and mucked everything up.

Bell: "The side mirror is out of position."

Nolan: "He might have bumped it when he climbed out, or grabbed it to steady himself."

Bell: "Maybe. And I don't like the open door, he would have closed it. You don't waste AC out here."

Nolan: "Maybe he wanted to keep listening to his music. He was drunk."

Bell: "Jeremiah was a drinker, not a drunk. And no hard stuff till after sundown."

Nolan: "How often did you see McLemore during daylight hours?"

Bell: "Not very."

Nolan: "Then how do you know?"

Bell: "Cuz he told me, that was his rule."

Nolan: "Could be he made an exception. If all this was staged for our benefit, where is the evidence that another party came and went? I don't see any footprints or tire tracks."

The immediate area was a thin layer of sandy soil atop a bed of reddish rock, patches of which shone through like a balding scalp.

Bell: "If someone went to all this trouble to set the scene they wouldn't just jump in their four-wheeler and peel out. They'd drive the Jeep here with the corpse in the bed, unwrap the body, stage the scene and walk off to a waiting vehicle."

Nolan: "What about footprints?"

Bell: "You see them big cold mountains up 'ere, Lieutenant? They suck up the heat from the desert floor which makes for a lotta wind. They could drag a piece of brush behind 'em as they left and let the wind do the rest."

Nolan: "Sounds plausible. Any suggestions?"

Bell: "Billy Chickenplucker. He's got some real Injun name but that's what everybody calls him. He's pureblood Paiute, can track anything that moves."

Nolan: "What's his secret?"

Bell: "Don't know. But last Feb we had some space cadets from Frisco camped out at the river. Their five-year-old son wandered off when they were gettin' the load on. Dipshits didn't call us till that night but Billy tracked that boy down on a cloudy moonless night. Took his time but he went right to him."

Nolan: "Great."

Bell: "I didn't say we found him alive."

Nolan: "Oh."

Bell: "Ha, gotcha! The boy was froze solid but still breathin'. Desert turns cold quick as it turns hot that time of year, something to do with the dry air, lack of molecules and so forth. They say the dark side of the moon is a zillion degrees colder than the bright side."

Nolan: "Didn't know that."

Bell: "Learn something new every day, that's my motto."

Nolan: "How did Billy track him down in the dead of night?"

Bell: "No clue."

Nolan: "You must have some idea."

Bell: "Well, he's got a schnozz like a bloodhound, Billy does, but the wind dies down after dark so how's he gonna smell something that's a mile away?"

Nolan: "Maybe he smelled his trail."

Bell: "Ten hours later on a windy day? Don't think so. The boy was a-whimperin' when we found him, too weak to call out. But, same deal, how do you hear a whimper from a mile away?"

Nolan: "Did Billy repeatedly hush you and the other officers?"

Bell: "Yeah, I think so."

Nolan: "There's your answer."

Bell: "I'll be damned. But how's an Indian tracker with super-keen hearing gonna help us here?"

Nolan: "You're the one who brought him up."

Bell: "Shit, just thought of something."

Nolan: "What that?"

Bell: "If Jer stepped out to take a piss he would've lowered his fly in the air- conditioned comfort of his truck."

Nolan: "His fly being up or down is not going to prove anything. He might have lowered it once he got outside."

Bell: "Don't think so. He's only two steps from his truck and it's blowy here in the daytime."

Nolan: "You're suggesting McLemore would have moved further away to make sure he didn't get any piss on his truck?"

Bell: "Affirmative. I'm guessin' he took two steps and fell over. I'll just roll him over and...oh shit. You have never seen so many fire ants."

Nolan: "Meaning, I suppose, that McLemore has his fly down."

Bell: "If that's a joke, Lieutenant, fuck you."

Nolan: "Apologies, officer. It's my way of card filing it."

Bell: "Your what?"

Nolan: "Processing it, filing it away."

Bell: "Filing what away?"

Nolan: "Horrible stuff, like you see in police work. Or war."

Bell: "You serve in Korea?"

Nolan: "World War Two."

Bell: "No shit, you don't look old enough."

Nolan: "I was a young un."

Bell: "Man, I would've killed to see some action in the Big One."

Nolan: "Sure. It was a lot of fun."

Bell and I returned to Clovis in the helicopter and described what we had seen. Clovis insisted on seeing for himself and it took both Bell and me to restrain the little man.

Bell: "You don't wanna see it, Clovis, trust me."

Boudreaux settled down eventually. Bell suggested that JM's death had been staged as an accident. I countered that we had not observed any footprints or tire tracks at the scene.

Clovis choppered us over the surrounding area, explaining what Bell had already mentioned, that the constant wind made footprints and tire tracks hard to come by.

Clovis: "But greasewood bushes and cholla cactus are slow-growing. They take weeks to heal over if scraped or cracked. The safest route for a truck would be a dry lake bed or...shitabrick, look at that!"

Nolan: "What?"

Clovis: "Hard for you to see maybe but that's the footprint of a Bell-47, rotor wash pattern to boot. Nobody local has a Bell-47."

Clovis landed nearby. We examined the dry and dusty lakebed. The imprint of the chopper was hard to see. But the indent of the landing bars was half an index-finger deep.

I knew this was a significant discovery. The imprint looked recent and was within a hundred yards of the Jeep.

The next order of business was to search for evidence that someone had crossed from the Jeep to the landing spot.

Bell: "We need to call Billy."

Nolan: "How do we do that?"

Bell: "On the radiator phone."

Nolan: "The who?"

Bell: "You'll see."

Clovis flew us to a lonely phone booth on a stretch of dirt road in the middle of nowhere. It is called the radiator phone because it was placed there as a lifeline for tourists with overheated vehicles.

Bell dialed 0, identified himself and flirted with the operator for a longer time than this parched investigator would have liked. At long last Bell said he needed to speak to Billy Chickenplucker. The operator seemed to know who that was.

Bell: "This is important police business, Arlene, so no listenin' in."

The mini-cassette recorder did not pick up her reply but I remember overhearing an insulted 'Of course not.'

Billy Chickenplucker joined us at the radiator phone in short order, driving a green Karmann Ghia. Billy was not an American Indian from central casting. He was short and plump, wore wire rim glasses, a purple and white tie-dyed shirt, and a rainbow bandana wrapped around his head.

He joined us as we choppered back to our original landing point, then walked to the Jeep. Clovis didn't ask to come along this time.

Billy took in the grisly scene with a cool eye. We told him we suspected that someone had walked away from the Jeep but we didn't indicate any particular direction. Billy walked in a wide circle and scanned the ground as we watched and waited. He pulled a pressurized can from his satchel and sprayed it on several flat rocky surfaces.

Bell: "Is that a can of Pledge?"

Billy: "You know about desert varnish, doncha?"

Bell: "Guess not."

Billy: "It's a shiny dark brown coating on rocks resulting from the interaction between iron, manganese and intense heat. Pledge does the same thing with rubber."

Bell: "Huh?"

Billy: "It interacts with any trace of rubber subjected to intense heat."

Bell: "You sayin' you see footprints?"

Billy: "Yassuh. Now you're gonna say most folks wear leather-soled boots in the desert to stomp rattlesnakes and that's true, but most leather boots these days got these rubber plugs in the heels that act as shock absorbers. That's what my spray-on Pledge brings up."

Billy was able to trace a single set of footsteps for about forty yards in the direction of the helicopter landing imprint. We even spotted a full boot print on some crushed buffalo grass. I put my foot next to it and snapped a pic. But further on the rocky dirt turned to loose sand and we lost the trail.

Initial indications were that someone drove McLemore's corpse to the scene in the Willys Jeep, staged his death, then walked to a waiting helicopter and took off.

via Telex

TE# 3744019-j

N₀ 53448

30 May, 1968

TO: James J. Angleton, Chief of CI Staff,

              Clandestine Services, DDP

FROM: ROLLTOP

SUBJECT: Jeremiah McLemore

STATUS: **TOP SECRET**

CODING: TSJ-91

On May 29, using the legend Lieutenant Richard Nolan, U.S. Army, I accompanied Needles PD Officer Thomas A. Bell on a helicopter ride piloted by Clovis Boudreaux, a civilian who runs a private chopper service. The objective was to locate missing Camp X trash hauler Jeremiah McLemore. Both Bell and Boudreaux were friends of the missing subject.

Boudreaux suggested we look in a remote desert spot where they had often enjoyed drinking beer and target shooting. Boudreaux theorized that McLemore might have gone to this favored spot to unwind before his meeting with Officer Bell re: McLemore's being offered money by a "suspicious stranger" to divulge information about his trash pickups at Camp X. Bell said that McLemore told him the stranger introduced himself as "Wendell".

WHAT WE FOUND

McLemore's Willys Jeep was indeed parked in the favored spot with the driver's door winged open. A body savaged by wildlife to the point of unrecognizability lay a few steps from the Jeep. Ofc. Bell recognized the body's clothing as belonging to his friend. Pending confirmation by the San Bernardino County Coroner, the logical assumption is that the corpse is McLemore.

No signs of a second or third party were immediately evident at the scene. When we got airborne in Boudreaux's chopper, however, the pilot claimed to see the faint landing imprint of a Bell-47 a short distance away. A closer examination of the site confirmed this claim.

Officer Bell summoned a Paiute Indian tracker of his acquaintance who was able to detect recent boot tracks leaving the scene, heading in the direction of the helicopter landing imprint.

PRELIMINARY CONCLUSION

Jeremiah McLemore, a Korean War deserter, was so unnerved by his impending interrogation by authorities, that he consumed too much marijuana and alcohol, stepped out of his air-conditioned truck to urinate and was felled by the blistering heat. Daytime temperatures at this time of year routinely top one hundred and ten degrees.

SECONDARY CONCLUSION

Jeremiah McLemore was killed by an untraceable poison or suffocation and the scene was staged by Soviet Bloc agents or subcontractors to make it appear an accidental death.

McLemore was a 'desert rat', accustomed to the brutal heat because he worked outdoors during the daytime. The boot prints moving away from the scene and toward the Bell-47 landing imprint strongly suggest other players in his demise. Initial speculation includes the possibility McLemore was killed elsewhere, most likely at his home where he lived alone, and his body wrapped in a tarp and transported to the scene in the back of his Jeep.

CAVEATS TO SECONDARY CONCLUSION

The Bell-47 is a high-profile helicopter that would attract notice in this small community. As pilot Boudreaux said, "Nobody local has a Bell-47."

This is not to say that it could not have been hired in Las Vegas or San Bernardino, both of which are within the Bell-47's flight range, if refueling was provided upon landing.

The question is, why would a Soviet Bloc intelligence agency risk such a flashy 'James Bond' maneuver when simpler means of egress from the death scene were available to their hired hands? A four-wheel drive vehicle would have sufficed.

In addition, I do not believe that an operation of this complexity would have been attempted absent a capable independent local liaison; someone with intimate knowledge of the terrain, the roads and the routines of local law enforcement.

And knowledge of McLemore's habits as well. How else would enemy intelligence have known about Jeremiah McLemore's favorite spot in the Mojave Desert?

FINAL CONCLUSION

None available at this time.

::TRANSMISSION COMPLETE::

via Telex

TE# 3744019-j

N₀ 53509

3 June 1968

TO: ROLLTOP

FROM: James J. Angleton, Chief of CI Staff,

           Clandestine Services, DDP

SUBJECT: Jeremiah McLemore

STATUS: **TOP SECRET**

CODING: TSJ-91

As for the forensic conclusions of your Paiute Indian tracker and the local helicopter pilot I maintain a healthy skepticism. The PNA team deemed your photos of the boot print and the Bell-47 landing imprint "inconclusive."

In addition, I note that the findings of the Needles Police Department report do not corroborate your own.

I understand and appreciate that your innate bulldog tenacity will prompt you to investigate further, perhaps in an extralegal manner. Pray remember that we are far afield here. Our charter does not permit interference with domestic law enforcement in the conduct of a criminal investigation.

PRELIMINARY CONCLUSION

Keep the bulldog on a short leash for now.

::TRANSMISSION COMPLETE::

My darling girl,

You sounded a little blue on the telephone though I couldn't get you to admit it. I don't expect you to be sunny and bright all the time. Just because I idolize you doesn't mean you have live up to it. You're entitled to be human, occasionally.

A couple of quick stories to cheer you up. The local cop I'm working with is 21 years old, tall, gangly and quick-witted. I'll call him Ned. I was doing a ride-along on Route 66 with him to get the lay of the land when we saw a young male hitchhiker. Ned pulled over and approached the man. I listened from the squad car.

Ned asked the man when he went AWOL. (That's Army talk for Absent Without Leave.) The young man furiously denied that he was a member of the "United States Pig Military."

Ned gave him a quick once over and said, drolly, "You've got a buzz cut. It's 110 degrees and you're wearing spit-shined brogans, a starched and pressed t-shirt and khaki slacks. So I'm going to ask you again. When did you go AWOL?"

We ended up running him back to the 29 Palms Marine Base instead of calling the MP's. That's about a hundred miles, but it took only two hour's round trip. They drive fast out here.

The locals seem happy despite the heat. Early today I passed a fellow on the sidewalk as I set off in quest of coffee. (Imagine a motel where you can't get a morning cup o' joe.) The fellow was whistling, no particular tune, just whistling as he walked on down the road. If we approached someone doing that in D.C. we would cross the street.

Good news, there is blue here besides copper tailings. This evening, through a thin haze of contrails, I saw the far off purple peaks somehow bleed into the rays of the setting sun to create a blazing neon blue-red sunset that you, my love, would not believe.

I will be home soon, I promise, God willing and the creek don't rise. With kisses to you and our beloved Helen, I sign myself,

Your devoted swain

My dearest husband,

You are burdened with important work so I am
reluctant to bother you with a very difficult question: What is
to become of this country?

I shall never forget that terrible Friday in April when we
stood on our balcony, watching the black sky turn to orange as
Washington burned. And now this. Will we burn again?

This America I have dreamed about since girlhood, this
land of astronauts and movie stars, of John Kennedy and
Martin Luther King. And now this. Another Kennedy brother
murdered, another man of righteousness shot dead. In the
name of St. Patrick the Apostle, I cannot understand it. Do
they not know they live in God's own paradise?

Do you remember? Our Helen touched Bobby Kennedy's hand at a rally in May. She has his campaign poster pinned inside the door of her bedroom.

She will not be consoled. How am I ever to explain to her what has happened when I cannot explain it to myself?

You are wise about the world of politics. Please help us to make sense of this wickedness.

Your loving wife,

L

Notes to myself, 06/06/68:

It is my belief that Jeremiah McLemore was approached by a KGB officer because they had discovered he was a U.S. Army deserter. (It would have been inconceivable to them that JM got only 14 mos. and a dishonorable discharge. Red Army deserters get a cigarette and a blindfold.) The KGB officer would have arranged to have JM's phone tapped prior to the approach in order to determine if he squealed to authorities after the contact.

I was pretty certain McLemore was the victim of a KGB hit. Such drastic action on foreign soil meant that the approach came from a VIP asset, a well-established KGB officer under deep cover. But why risk a VIP to recruit a garbage man? The only answer that made any sense was that the Sovs were desperate to penetrate that gray steel building.

I invited Ofc. Bell to my motel for beer and pizza after sweeping the room for bugs. There was a nagging possibility I needed to clear up. Or two.

The guns-drawn hostility between CIA and FBI has diminished over the course of my twenty-year career. They were still burrheads with thick necks and we - or my colleagues anyway - were still pipe-smoking Yalies in tweed jackets.

We call them Fan Belt Inspectors. Not to be outdone, the FBI refer to us counterintelligence operators – whose job it is to prevent enemy penetration - as HI's. Hymen inspectors.

But we have come to realize the need to work together. The Cuban Missile Crisis and the assassination of JFK made our intramural squabbles look dumb.

Which is not to say that J. Edgar Hoover doesn't still hate our guts.

I have a long-standing FBI contact who keeps me updated provided I do likewise. Seems the feds had questioned Ofc. Bell about his best buddy Bob Reese. Reese was a 26-year-old NPD officer who resigned abruptly four months ago.

A subsequent string of sophisticated robberies of banks and retail establishments that involved the robber concealing himself inside the business overnight led the FBI to suspect Reese, who had shown particular aptitude on rob/burg investigations. Bell informed them he hadn't seen or heard from Reese since he quit the force.

I had a plan in mind for Mr. Reese but could not risk putting his name in the CIA Persons of Interest hopper, which would eventually spit it out on top of Mount Jimbo, as the inbox on Angleton's desk is known. I would have to wait for the results of the FBI's probe of Reese.

I did Bell the courtesy of placing my portable cassette tape recorder with the plug-in mike on the coffee table.

Here is the transcript, dated 06/05/1968:

B: "What, your cigarette pack is low on batteries?"

N: "No comment."

B: "You know, Lieutenant, if you wanted to sell that scam you should have smoked a cig once in a while."

N: "I know, I hate the damn things. My old man died of lung cancer and it wasn't pretty."

B: "Sorry to hear that."

N: "And you have my word any tapes I make are strictly for my own use, to keep the facts straight."

B: "You're not shipping 'em back to D.C.?"

N: "Nope."

B: "Well, feel free to use 'em at a big Senate hearing someday. I could use the publicity."

N: "Ha ha. Now, officer, a serious question. Do you think there's any chance Jeremiah McLemore committed suicide?"

B: "Stupid serious question."

N: "Why is that?"

B: "He had the baddest ass truck in the county."

N: "Having nice stuff doesn't really mean much at the end of the day."

B: "Yeah, it's the hunt, not the kill, I get it. But Jer was still in hot pursuit. Just last week he was all excited, he had a lead on a water pump that would restore his Willys to 100% mint condition. Excited about a dumbass water pump! That sound like a suicide vic to you?"

N: "No, it doesn't."

B: "I heard something about a beer."

N: "Coming right up."

I got us two cold Miller High Lifes from the mini-fridge.

N: "You don't look happy, officer."

B: "I prefer Mescan beer."

N: "I'll keep that in mind. Now, how could they have killed Jeremiah so quickly after his call to you. I'm assuming they tapped his phone."

B: "Who's they?

N: "Soviet officers or agents."

B: "Christ. How do they usually do it?"

N: "Lethal injection of an untraceable poison."

B: "Christ. Well, Jer was strong for a short guy, wiry. That'd take three men. Two to hold him down, one to shoot him up."

N: "They don't use a hypodermic, it's more like a dart. But it leaves a tiny mark that a sharp coroner might notice."

B: "San Berdoo's got a sharp coroner. So, how?"

N: "Most likely a strongman smothered him with a rag soaked in chloroform. Then wrapped him in a tarp, carried him to the Jeep and drove off in the dead of night.

B: "It'd have to be dead of night cause everyone knows Jer doesn't loan out his truck."

N: "And any signs of trauma from a struggle would be long gone by the time his body was found."

B: "We looking for one suspect? Guy who contacted Jer also killed him in his bed?"

N: "I don't think so, different job descriptions. They would have used a contractor for the hit."

B: "Why?"

H: "Imagine the shitstorm if a KGB officer gets arrested for murdering an American citizen on American soil."

B: "So we're looking for two suspects?"

N: "Might be three. We're not likely to find the KGB officer, same for the assassin. They would have been in and out in no time. And that's a job for the FBI and the Bureau of Customs. That leaves us with their local liaison, the guy who knows the ropes."

B: "Could this local yokel be the killer?"

N: "Could be, but that's not how it works most times. We need to find the local yokel and work backwards. Anyone come to mind?"

B: "I'm a rookie cop who breaks up bar fights."

N: "I was wondering if it might be Bob Reese. Did he have any pro-Soviet sympathies?"

B: "Bob Reese? Bob Reese couldn't find Russia on a map, and Russia's big! And how'd you know about Bob Reese?"

N: "I know the FBI questioned you about him because you were close pals."

B: "Only the dickhead took a powder and didn't say why."

N: "I ask because a KGB officer or contract killer wouldn't know about McLemore's favorite spot in the desert. That's local knowledge, something Bob Reese might know."

B: "Plus a dozen other people."

N: "Sure."

B: "Here's what you need to know about Bob Reese. I was just a couple weeks on the job, had my first solo d&d call – that is, esteemed members of the Committee, cop talk for drunk and disorderly."

N: "Esteemed who?"

B: "Members of the big deal Senate committee yer going to play this tape for someday."

N: "Oh. Of course."

B: "So it's sunset at the Red Dog Saloon and it's a fucking John Ford movie. I walk in, it looks empty. The setting sun splashes my silhouette against the back wall. I can barely see the barkeep, who greets me in a low voice, but I don't see anyone at the bar till the door swings shut behind me. Ka-dunk.

It's dark in the Red Dog, they like it that way. When my eyeballs adjust I see it's Kenny the black guy, a sweetheart most days but now he's had him one too many. The barkeep's cut him off but he's got a death grip on the lip below the bar. Plus he's a karate instructor.

I'm a rookie, I don't wanna call for backup 'less I have to. But Kenny, he ain't leaving without some kickass.

Bob Reese is off duty, drinkin' beer and listenin' to the police scanner. When he hears me call it in, he runs – he doesn't have a car – he runs eight blocks from his apartment to the Red Dog to assist in Kenny the black guy's arrest and apprehension."

N: "Impressive."

B: "Damn straight."

N: "I sense a punch line."

B: "Sometimes, when you got beer, you don't need gasoline."

N: "Good one, officer.

Now, it seems to me there are two lines of inquiry here that look promising. First one is tracing back the Bell-47 to see who rented it; the 47 has a flight range of about 250 miles. Cut that in half for the round trip and we're looking at commercial airports within 125 miles."

B: "That's dumb. I mean, choppers can take off and land anyplace flat, and we've got plenty of flat around here. And, hey, if they wanted to be really slick, they'd land the 47 in the middle of nowhere, collapse the rotors and haul it back in a semi to anywhere USA."

N: "Hadn't thought of that. Maybe using a chopper as a getaway vehicle does make sense: no tire tracks, which is what cops would be looking for. It was just dumb luck Clovis saw the landing imprint."

B: "And what's that second line of inquiry?"

N: "That's trickier. It involves breaking the law."

B: "Maybe you should turn off that tape recorder now, Lieutenant."

I did that, tho I had anticipated this possibility and kept my cigarette pack mini-cassette going as backup. I realize that this was reprehensible behavior on my part, but that is what we spies do. We spy.

N: "The second line of inquiry is to break into JM's house and look for evidence of a phone tap."

B: "Couldn't they tap it at the pole?"

N: "Too public. They'd need a phone company truck with a cherry picker."

B: "What about a listening bug, ya know, stuck in a lamp, under a table?"

N: "No, they'd want both sides of any phone calls.

What I'm thinking, provided the FBI probe of Mr. Reese comes up empty, is that I could recruit Reese to help me do a b&e. To act as lookout."

B: "Why not me?"

N: "I wouldn't want to ruin your career."

B: "Go ahead, ruin it. I only took this gig to pay back Moms, plus drive cars well in excess of the posted limit. I'm not gonna be here a year from now no matter what."

N: "What's your plan?"

B: "Stash some cash and return to Sacto. There's a new morning jock at KXOA who's kickin' butt. His name is

Don Imus. I plan to be his gofer for no money and get my foot in the door."

N: "You'd be good on the radio."

B: "But..."

N: "Well, believe it or not, I was famous for a brief time twenty years ago."

B: "What for?"

N: "We've only got one six pack, officer."

B: "I'll bring a case next time."

N: "Good idea. Point is you'd be amazed how quickly it passes. Best quote I've heard on the subject was from Horace Greeley, the famous newspaperman. 'Fame is a vapor.'"

B: "And you're still quoting him a hundred years later."

N: "Sure, but Greeley reinvented himself many times."

B: "What's your point?"

N: "You're a good cop. You don't want to slam that door shut at twenty-one years old."

My darling girl,

If only I could help you to make sense of this wickedness. I can only tell you that the man who shot Bobby Kennedy is a Palestinian who was angry that RFK was pro-Israel. He may just as well have assassinated any other candidate of either party because they all share the same position. Which is to tell you precisely nothing useful in making sense of the hatred and violence that is convulsing our country in this dreadful year.

Do not fret. There will not be another riot in D.C. Just a great sadness.

I recall a malt shop date back when I was a boy of sixteen or so. The war had already begun in Europe but we Yanks were doing our level best to ignore it. My date — her name was Rebecca, I think — asked me a profound question, seeking reassurance.

"I believe that human beings are basically good. Don't you agree?"

She was a peach of a girl, a sunny, blue-eyed Presbyterian in a town of dour, dark-eyed Catholics. I agreed with her. Human beings are basically good. Oddly enough, despite all I have seen, I still believe that.

I think the caveat is this: When everyday people feel they have no control over their daily lives, they will turn, slowly but surely, to sly monsters who promise them redemption. Have we reached that point in America? I don't think so. But putting that question in writing is not something I had ever imagined doing.

Perhaps I can coax a smile by recounting some of the goings on in this odd little burg. For instance, the headline in this morning's Needles Desert Star was "The Toulmuns Return from Norway."

Below the fold was a large photo of Patrick 'Pancho' O'Keefe, wearing a droopy mustache, a goofy grin and an enormous sombrero, pouring margaritas for the local hospital's Fundraising Fiesta.

The only sign that this wasn't Anytown USA was the weather box in the lower right-hand corner of the front page. High: 115 Low: 88 Humidity: 8%.

I have been spending time with the local cops, quite a colorful bunch. Their favorite diner adjoins a gas station, Fancher's Shell, which is owned by, of all people, the County

Coroner. Fancher's specialty is chicken fried steak, but the cops don't call it that. When the craggy waitress comes over to take their order, as she has done one hundred times before, they stroke their chins.

"Now Mabel," they say, "I see to where the coroner had a good crop this week, so I'm a-thinkin' to have me the cadaver cutlets."

This causes them to wheeze and get teary-eyed with mirth.

But that's not the funny part, not to me anyway. The funny part is the way Mabel gives them a weary look and sighs. "Don't you boys never git tired of tellin' that joke?"

Which cracks them up even more.

I find these small town rituals fascinating. And somehow reassuring.

Give our beloved Helen a tender kiss on her bony head and tell her I will be home as soon as humanly possible. When the time is right, I will arrange for the AG's office to send her a personal RFK memento.

I love you like a bird loves spring,

H

My dearest husband,

I am, at heart, a deeply silly person. That is why I so envy you the experience of ordering cadaver cutlets at Fancher's Shell.

You were right, of course. We did not have another riot here after the murder of RFK, just a great sadness. After so much heartbreak these last five years no one knows what else to say, we have worn out all the soothing words. The routine comings and goings of everyday life are all that is left to hear.

It seems to me that America needs a LEADER in its time of trial and tribulation, yet I see no sign of him. President Johnson was a courageous champion of Negro rights who will be celebrated in history books. But he can no longer lead because, as that famous political cartoon has shown, Viet Nam is tattooed on his stomach.

The presidential candidates fail to inspire me, though I will confess to a schoolgirl crush on longshot Eugene McCarthy. He has an Irish twinkle about him. But Hubert H. Humphrey and Richard M. Nixon? Are these the best leaders that this country of utmost importance has to offer?

Please do not bother to try and answer this question, Mo Ghrá. Tis a mystery for the ages.

Your loving wife,

L

Notes to myself, 06/11/1968:

I had a slap-my-forehead moment when an obvious question popped into my head - why in the world would the Soviets risk soliciting Jeremiah McLemore when all they had to do was sift thru his truck's dump site to find what they wanted?

I couldn't believe such an obvious thing had been overlooked, but I work for one of the world's largest bureaucracies so you never know. I drove the hundred miles to 29 Palms Marine Base to make sure. Jim Angleton and I had an arrangement: he would do his best to be available any weekday to take my call at precisely 3 p.m. PST, should the need arise. I called him at that time on the KY-3 and asked the question.

He snorted.

I should probably explain about the KY-3. It's a voice encryption system, what we used to call a scrambled line. It uses Pulse Code Modulation, which is a way to 'digitize' samples of sound waves and make them into a series of numbers that are gibberish if they're intercepted.

The KY-3 is the first secure phone system to use transistors instead of hot and bulky vacuum tubes. It's about the size of a small fridge and has a rotary handset - a big improvement on its WWII granddad, the SIGSALY, which required a refrigerated room and weighed over 50 tons.

I wanted a recording of this conversation, tho I wasn't sure why.

The National Security Agency spent millions to develop the KY-3. It was supposed to prevent a 'man in the middle', a term we use to indicate an eavesdropper. But what if the man in the middle was in the breast pocket of my sports coat.

I knew the KY-3 setup had an audio booth for privacy, with a glass door so the technician could make sure no unauthorized tape recording was taking place. But that setup had been designed before the invention of the mini-recorder. The question was how to hold the handset so that the mini-mike in my breast pocket would pick up the audio from the KY-3 handset w.out calling attention to myself.

'Anticipation deflects confrontation' was a constant maxim at spy school. Prep the scene properly and you won't face difficult questions.

I winced in pain and rolled my head around when I met the KY-3 technician at 29 Palms, said I had a crick in my neck that wouldn't quit.

And that is how, while contorted like Quasimodo, my head canted low and left, I came to record the following conversation with James Angleton on 06/10/1968.

I captured most of it:

A: "Ah, my good and trusted friend, I have always said to colleagues who doubt your perspicacity because you lack a sheepskin, Officer Schroeder is akin to St. Thomas Aquinas, dubbed 'the dumb ox' by classmates for his habit of asking questions."

My cigarette pack mini-recorder missed the next part as I rearranged myself into a more tolerable position, but I remember that Angleton said that it was part of the deception. I asked what he meant.

A: "We gave McLemore an elaborate dumping regimen involving several abandoned mines on federal land. The dumping was done during daylight hours and the choice of sites was random. The only discernible pattern was that when McLemore did his sole late night trash pickup once a week he would dump the load at an abandoned thorium mine with an orange metal sign that read in reflective letters: 'Danger – Radioactive Materials'. This was meant to bait the hook."   c

N: "Did they bite?"

All I captured here was "some play on the line" but, as I remember it, Angleton indicated they did not bite.

N: "Meaning no evidence of KGB or surrogates attempting to explore the radioactive mine? I assume you had onsite surveillance cameras."

A: "No surveillance cameras. We didn't expect them to explore a radioactive mineshaft in the middle of the Mojave Desert. We expected the KGB would make an overture to Army deserter and war protestor Jeremiah McLemore instead."

N: "Did they?"

A: "That is what I have dispatched you to Satan's Notch to find out."

Well. It was nice of JJA to tell his good and trusted friend of these elaborate arrangements. He would say it was a test, to see if I was still paying attention. Fair enough. Stress and office politics take their toll. At twenty years on I was an old timer, ready for pasture.

Only I wasn't. I have always considered myself a late
bloomer. At 46 I felt like I was just coming into my own.

As for Angleton's good and trusted friend remark, I took
that w. a grain of salt. I cherished it because I knew he was
stingy w. compliments. I questioned it for the same reason.

Was he giving me the softsoap so I'd be more pliable to
unreasonable demands? Of course he was, every boss does
that. But at the end of the day I took him at his word.

My darling girl,

There is something crystal clear about this place. Searing heat in the daytime that concentrates the senses, a billion stars at night. A perfect imprint of a woman's face in a stack of pancakes.

Allow me to explain...

I was riding night patrol with Officer Ned when he got a drunk-in-public call at Sambo's, a local restaurant. We rolled up to find a heavyset woman face down in her stack of buttermilk pancakes. When Ned gently lifted up her head, she left behind a precise imprint of her nose, cheeks and forehead.

This drew a ripple of mirth from the staff but Ned quickly called for an ambulance. Turns out he has a diabetic aunt with a sweet tooth and he diagnosed a diabetic coma. If he had thrown this woman in the drunk tank that night she would have died.

I see so much of my young self in these brash young men out here, though they are more mature and true blue than I was at their age. I find them a breath of fresh air after the pall of D.C. cynicism.

Okay. Fresh air may be the wrong choice of words. Stepping out the door at midday here is like smacking a brick wall at fifty miles an hour.

I love you always and forever.

Tell Helen I miss her birdy laugh,

H

P.S. I can hear your insistent curiosity churning from 3000 miles away: If she had her face buried in a stack of pancakes, why wasn't this woman already dead of asphyxiation? The only explanation I can conjure is that Sambo's whips a lot of air into their pancakes.

P.P.S. And, yes, here's my suggestion for a new Sambo's slogan: "Pancakes so fluffy, you can pass out in them!"

Notes to myself, 06/13/68:

My FBI contact reported that Bob Reese was clean as a peeled egg; no Comsymph activity and no evidence of participation in local robberies. In fact, due to the solid tradecraft of the perpetrator, there was barely any evidence to speak of.

It didn't look as if Reese was an ideological recruit but that didn't mean much. Most contractors are mercenaries. The Sovs prefer it that way; they don't have to worry about a recruit refusing a command because it doesn't precisely square with his reading of socialist dogma. And Reese had all the things they would be looking for – local knowledge, martial skills, and an apparent willingness to break the law.

My photo of the boot print at the death scene was the only hard evidence I had re: JM's killer. I had placed my size elevens next to the print to get an approx on their size. They were shorter, size 9 or so.

I explained this to Bell at one of our beer and pizza recording sessions on 06/12/68.

(I get the sense Bell doesn't have a TV because he is usually keen to stay late and watch. It's a cinch to get him Wednesday night when Have Gun Will Travel is on. But he's also partial to Fridays and The Dean Martin Show.)

B: "You think Bob Reese would kill a drinking buddy?"

N: "I need to make sure he didn't."

B: "How?"

N: "I need to determine his shoe size. Does the PD provide footwear?"

B: "Ha. You get a uniform, a nightstick and a snub-nose .38, which is useless as tits on a boar hog."

N: "So you buy your own gun belt and boots."

B: "Yes sir. And a .357 magnum if you know what's good for you."

N: "Where?"

B: "Claypool's, in town. Bob Reese wore cowboy boots."

I went to Claypool's the following day without much hope the store would keep records of a customer's shoe size. I told the eager young clerk I wanted to give my pal Bob Reese a new pair of cowboy boots for his birthday. To my surprise the clerk rifled thru some card files and came up with Reese's shoe size, then mentioned that Reese's birthday wasn't till October.

I asked how he knew that. His reply was memorable:

"Claypool's sends a birthday greeting to all our customers. It includes a 25% discount coupon good only on their special day."

Score one for small town merchants. Reese's shoe size was 13. He hadn't killed his drinking buddy.

Bell and I set off to find Bob Reese that evening, Saturday, about six p.m. Our first stop was The Rails, his old hangout near the RR junction, to ask the regulars if they had seen him. Bell groaned when we entered.

"Shit, it's Big Ray."

An enormous man in overalls was sitting at the right end of the bar. The rest of the stools held a ragtag group of men who were squirming and looking uncomfortable. Bell went to the barkeep to ask what was going on.

"Big Ray is buying rounds for the house." I noted that Ray's .45 lay on the bar in front of him.

In a whisper the barkeep explained. "But he won't let em' go to the bathroom."

Ray looked over his shoulder in our direction and raised his mug. "Drink up, boys."

"OK, Ray, fun's over," said Bell. "Put up the gun."

Ray glared at Bell and slid his hand closer to the .45.

Things were about to go south – Big Ray lit to the gills, rookie cop out to prove himself – so I shot my mouth off.

I challenged Big Ray to an arm wrestling contest: winner stays, loser goes home.

Big Ray thought this a fine idea.

I had never arm wrestled with a full bladder before but I imagined it might affect your concentration. In other words, I didn't need to pin Big Ray. I just needed to hold on long enough for him to bolt to the men's room. I cheated by wrapping my legs around the bottom of the barstool.

Little known fact about arm wrestling - it's as much about bone as muscle, the wrist bone being the fulcrum. I calculated my wrist was thick as Big Ray's was beneath the suet.

Bell counted us down, 3-2-1.

I got a good jump and leaned in for all I was worth, even thought for a moment I might beat him flat out. But Big Ray stopped me cold about halfway down. And then he started back up.

We locked eyes. His were gray as granite where they weren't bloodshot, and they didn't look worried.

I cranked every erg of energy in my corkscrewed body into my right wrist, and still Ray's arm inched higher.

I'm supposed to be good at ju jitsu, where you use your opponent's energy against him. Hard to do when you're planted on a barstool. But there was no way I could lose this contest and maintain any credibility in this manly town.

When we were back to twelve noon, I tried something - I dropped my determined grimace and gave Big Ray a big shit-eating grin.

That confused him for an instant. An instant I used to make one last lunge.

I budged him about two inches but it didn't take. My little ploy had pissed off the human Brahma bull. My shoulder bone struggled to pop out of its socket. I was cooked.

It was right about then that the dam broke. Apparently Big Ray's fury at my cheap ploy had distracted him from his swollen bladder.

In any event, he let loose a torrent that cascaded out both legs of his overalls and soaked his work boots, causing the rapt bar patrons to erupt in laughter, and run off to the mens room.

Big Ray pocketed his .45 and stumbled out, head down.

I don't know if my spy school instructor would call it ju jitsu exactly, but things worked out.

Notes to myself, 06/17/68:

Doing shoe leather investigation in a small town is easy duty; there's only one of everything, maybe two.

Bell and I went to the only optician in town, Bell in uniform tho he was off duty. We would have needed a subpoena to demand medical records so Bell turned on the charm. My cigarette pack recorder was acting up on that Monday so the following quote is an approx based on same day notes:

B: "I have lost touch with my good buddy Bob Reese since he resigned from the NPD, and I'm getting worried. I think he gets his glasses here. Can you check to see if he has changed his contact info?"

The lady behind the counter obediently fetched the records.

Bell told me the address was obsolete but he recognized the phone number. He used the reverse phone directory at the PD to obtain the address in Topock, AZ, which is just east of Needles, across the Colorado River.

We had a solid lead on Bob Reese. Now what?

I had gotten ahead of myself once again. James Jesus Angleton was a poet in his college days, an acolyte of Ezra Pound and T.S. Eliot. He loved wordplay. I had teased a glum chuckle out of him once when I described my unfortunate tendency to leap ahead as "putting Descartes before the hearse."

Bell and I had another beer and pizza recording session at my motel that evening. I'd bought a six pack of a Mexican beer. The rookie thanked me for the improved selection of cerveza, but informed me that Corona was supposed to be served with a slice of lime.

I had to sit thru an episode of "Adam 12" before we could talk. Bell said he had learned most of what he knew about police procedure from the show.

N: "If you have a face-to-face with Reese I would like to be there."

B: "Bob Reese. Everyone calls him Bob Reese like it's one name."

N: "And Bob Reese is not going to be happy to see a stranger."

B: "No, he's not."

N: "Bob Reese has nothing to fear from me. I'm an intelligence officer, I work for the Armed Forces Security Agency. Unless Bob Reese has committed treason, I have no powers of arrest. Can I count on you to tell him that?"

B: "Why?"

N: "To help us find out what really happened to Jeremiah McLemore."

B: (long pause) "All right. Is your real name Lt. Dick Nolan?"

N: "Insofar as you're concerned, yes."

70

Notes to myself, 06/18/68:

Bell and I drove to Topock after dark. The house stood out on a street of double-wides and modest homes. It had something you rarely see here because they are too hard to keep cool – a second floor.

A beat-up orange Datsun was parked in front, not a Bob Reese car. But there was a detached one-car garage at the end of the gravel driveway. We took a look.

The garage was padlocked, its small side window tar-papered over from inside. We crept up to the front door and listened. Soft music was playing, something Latin, guitars.

A pretty young Mexican girl answered the door after several knocks. She looked frightened. Two tall gringos at the door after dark did not bode well. The guitar music was no longer playing.

Bell told her he was Bob Reese's bueno amigo and asked if she had seen him.

Her 'no, no, no, no' gave her away. That and her tousled hair and smeared lipstick.

"Bob Reese, Bell. Get your ass down here."

When Reese shambled down the bare wood stairs in his boxers a minute later, cursing Bell and his bad timing, I had to blink. And again.

Bob Reese looked like Thomas Bell's five-year-older twin. Same 6'4" frame, same thick hair – Reese's black, Bell's brown. Both trim, Reese more muscular and filled out.

They also shared matching smartass expressions, till Bob Reese got a load of me.

It was then I noticed something odd about him. Reese had one brown eye and one green. I don't believe I'd ever seen that b4.

Bell asked Reese what he'd been up to. Reese shook him off.

Bell introduced me and said I was an Army intelligence officer looking into the death of Jeremiah McLemore. When Reese asked why, Bell suggested they step outside for a smoke. They did so. Bell in his tan chinos and short-sleeve button down shirt, Reese in his underwear. I stayed at the doorway with the young senorita.

Her name was Teresa and she smelled of hashish. She took me into a kitchen w. dirty dishes piled high and got me a beer with gold foil on the bottle. Bohemia. The big pot on the stove smelled awful good. Teresa must have seen my nose twitching.

"You are ongry?"

"Always," I replied. She smiled and spooned up a bowl of what looked like a hominy stew with chili peppers, onions and chunks of pork. She put the bowl on the small wooden table. It shimmered with pork fat and fairly begged me - who hadn't had a home cooked meal in weeks - to dive in. But Teresa shook her head.

She diced a quarter of an onion quick as a blink and pushed it to one side of the cutting board. She chopped up a leafy green herb I have since come to know as cilantro, then scraped it into the bowl. I raised my spoon.

"No, no."

I watched, my tongue hanging out, as she quartered a lime and squeezed it over the bowl.

"Now yoo can eat," she said, fetching me a paper towel.

One of the perks of working for the Agency is that you get to wine and dine. You have an unlimited expense account in order to recruit sources. And, if you're senior enough, you get to attend embassy receptions and state dinners done to the nines. Steak Diane, Lobster Newburg, champagne and caviar.

But I don't believe I have ever enjoyed a meal more than that humble bowl of stew in that dirty kitchen. Spicy, aromatic and deeply satisfying. I asked Teresa, juice drooling down my chin, what this magic stew was called.

"Poos-o-le," she purred. Pray forgive me, but I heard the echo of a ruder word.

Bell and Reese ambled in after a time, looking chummy. I had not sworn Bell to secrecy about any of our conversations. If I have learned anything in twenty years, it's that you don't win or keep recruits with half-truths. You keep classified information classified but you don't get cute with elaborate cover stories designed to win them over. That way you won't forget a crucial detail at the worst possible moment and expose your country to nuclear annihilation.

But more on that later.

Reese excused himself to go put on some clothes. Teresa busied herself in the kitchen. I turned to Bell.

"Well?"

"Bob Reese is interested, but you'll have to lose that thing," he said pointing to my breast pocket.

"OK."

"And he wants to know what it pays. He's cruisin' on fumes."

"Sure."

My unlimited expense account didn't extend to unauthorized recruits. I would have to pay cash. I always travel with six one hundred dollar bills, ironed flat and sewn into the insteps of my bedroom slippers.

Enemy agents and contract thugs have tossed my digs and sliced up my suits and even hacked open the heels of my brogans looking for microfilm hidey holes. But they've never paid my decrepit slippers the least attention.

I would keep a hundred for myself just in case. $500 should be plenty in a town where gas cost 25 cents a gallon and the Blue Plate Special at Fancher's Shell was a buck 59.

Bob Reese reappeared in weathered jeans, a blue cowboy shirt with snap buttons, sleeves rolled up, and shiny red cowboy boots.

"Kangaroo," said Reese off my admiring look.

"Nice."

Bell gave me the hairy eyeball and tapped his chest. Oh yeah.

I went out to the car and locked my cigarette pack mini-recorder in the glove compartment.

Back inside, I nursed my Bohemia as the boys killed a bottle of Mezcal, performing a ritual that involved putting salt in the crotch of their thumbs, licking it, downing a shot then biting a slice of lime. Whoever punked out before the bottle was empty had to eat the fermented worm at the bottom.

The worm had nothing to worry about; the fifth didn't last two hours.

We sat in a cramped living room with a stone hearth and black light posters of Jimi Hendrix and Big Brother and the Holding Company. A brass hash pipe sat within easy reach on a side table. But the young men contented themselves with rotgut while in the presence of The Man.

Funny how the young assume their covert vices are theirs alone. This over-thirty member of the establishment couldn't possibly recognize the distinctive, smoky sweet scent of blond Leb that saturated the room.

I had spent time working with smugglers in the Middle East and was familiar with the color code that extends across, what old hands at the Agency still call, the Near East.

Blond Leb, from Lebanon, is a mild narcotic comparable to good marijuana. Red Turk, from Turkmenistan, is a denser hash similar in potency to Thai stick, the powerful reefer now all the rage with the flower children.

Further east was the hard stuff - opiated Afghan brown, shipped in thin flat bricks. Bricks stamped with the Afghan royal seal were the most sought after.

On a dare years ago I ate a piece of Royal Afghan brown that was half the size of my thumb. It tasted like a mix of clay, tobacco and dark chocolate, and it had me orbiting Jupiter for the better part of a day.

It was a fascinating experience. I never knew I could feel such profound...not sure how to describe this...giddiness, physical power, and colorful, blazing images that made no sense but contained an enormous certainty.

But then the high wore off and the work continued.

Drugs do work now and then. A dose of sodium pentothal can sometimes expose a bogus walk-in defector. And someone in Julius Caesar's day coined the phrase, "In vino veritas," tho it has been my experience that drunks make the best bullshitters.

Point being I couldn't have told anyone anything of value when I was under the influence of opiated Afghan brown. I couldn't have told them my name.

I went to the kitchen at one point to jot down some notes on that evening's conversation between Thomas Bell, Bob Reese and yours truly. The following is not verbatim:

Reese asked what I wanted him to do. I said he was to help me break into Jeremiah's house and act as lookout while I tossed the place. Reese said he had never been to JM's house and asked about the layout. I told him what I'd observed when I drove out to case the one-story bungalow on a quiet residential street on the northern edge of town.

On the corner of the street, next to JM's house, was a boarded-up house. On the other side was a well-tended house with a flagpole in the front yard. No flag at night on my first visit, flag flying proudly on my visit the following morning. Retired military.

A low chain-link fence ringed the property in a town where fences were nonexistent. I saw a well-chewed tennis ball in the yard. JM's neighbor had a small dog that couldn't bound over a three-foot fence. Bad news all around. Small dogs are yappy and old folks tend to be light sleepers.

The good news was the boarded-up house had a driveway where we could park out of sight. And the house across the street had a pile of newspapers and advertising circulars cluttering the front step.

Reese asked what would happen if we got caught. I told him that we would both be arrested.

Reese: "You don't have some federal get-out-of-jail card?"

Nolan: "Not this time. I'm freelancing."

Reese: "But the boss man in D.C. will smooth out the wrinkles at some point."

Nolan: "He might. But if he has to throw the local authorities a bone, you're it."

This bit of straight talk surprised Reese, and won him over. That and the five-hundred -dollar payday. One hundred earnest money, the rest on completion. I told Bell to go powder his nose b4 I gave Reese a C note that smelled of foot powder.

The deal done, the three of us settled back for gentlemanly conversation. Bell handed me a frosty Bohemia, Teresa was neither seen nor heard. I told Reese to give her my highest compliments on the posole. Reese said he would do that, adding, "She's a drunkard's dream, that one."

A rude thing to say, but honest. Bell asked if Reese missed being a cop.

Reese: "I'll tell you what I miss. I miss driving to a hot call at sunrise, doing 120 mph on the wrong side of Route 66, oncoming traffic pulling to the shoulder when they see me coming, flying past the wage slaves in the right lane as they crawl their way to their bullshit jobs in San Berdoo or wherever. That's what I miss."

Bell asked Reese what made him quit.

Bob Reese told the story of young girl who got shot in the head with a .45 when a railroad worker forced her to orally copulate him.

Reese: "Here's what the asshole told me: 'I just wanted a blowjob, I din't mean to kill her. Everything just exploded all at once.'

          I looked down at her in the cab of his truck, this beautiful young girl, brown hair blowing in the breeze, back of her head blown off, and I knew I should feel something but I just didn't. And that's when I knew it was time to quit."

We plotted how to break into JM's house, knowing the NPD had already searched the place. A search in which Bell, as a rookie, did not take part.

Reese: "The good news is the cops wouldn't have tossed it like a crime scene. The warrant would authorize them to look for a suicide note, drugs that may have contributed to his death and an address book so they could contact his next of kin. And then they'd paw through his trash cuz that's what cops do."

Nolan: "Why is that good news?"

Reese: "The cops would've entered through the front door. A hit man would've entered through the back door, or a back window if he couldn't work the door lock. If he was carrying a stiff he'd definitely exit the back door."

Nolan: "Why does that matter?"

Reese: "If McLemore's like most guys he hasn't cleaned his kitchen floor in six months. If there's a trail of footprints coming in from the back door and deeper prints in the grease going out, we got something."

Nolan: "The deeper prints from carrying a stiff. But what if the cops have tromped all over the kitchen looking for contact info? Lot of folks keep phone numbers on their fridge."

Reese: "A possibility."

Bell: "Plus the investigating officers would want to make sure none of Jeremiah's beer went to waste."

Nolan: "No doubt. The biggest threat is the yappy dog next door. Any suggestions?

Reese: "I'll make a batch of doggie downers, meatballs laced with Seconal. I got a police scanner in my truck. I'll monitor the NPD frequency and come running if they blast out a four five nine. Were the blinds drawn?"

Nolan: "Yes, blinds were drawn."

Reese: "Then we've got cover going in. Where's the back door?"

Nolan: "On the driveway side, closer to the house with the dog."

Reese: "Shit. Any cover between JM's house and the house behind him?"

Nolan: "There is no house behind him. Jer's street is the last one in that stretch. His backyard is the Mojave Desert."

Reese: "Well, screw the street, that's our entry and exit point. No NPD 327 is gonna catch my four-wheel Bronco on the open dirt."

I am embarrassed to report that this solution had not occurred to me. Bob Reese's suggestion was first rate.

Nolan: "It looks like we've got all the bases covered."

Bell: "Don't say that, you'll jinx it."

Reese: "Bell's right. I guess now's a good time for my little say-so." (clears his throat) I was trolling Broadway after closing time a couple years ago, working solo. I see a young female on the sidewalk, she's being tailed by two young males about ten yards back. I stop and ask if she's with the two guys. She's not. I approach the men and ask for their ID's. They're drunk, but I can handle two drunks, do it all the time.

The drunkest one calls me a name and tries to kick me in the balls. I clock him a good one and he splays out. But I've got my hands full with the other one, he's a live wire.

They don't tell you this, but being tall is key in police work; the chokehold's your best friend. After dancing with this scrappy little scrote for a minute or two, I get my arm bar under his chin and shut his carotid just as another cop rolls up.

I've got the situation under control, but the new gink thinks it's a good idea to cuff the shithead while he's doing the chicken. Cop manages to cuff one wrist but the scrappy little scrote, spazzing from lack of oxygen, uses the loose cuff to lacerate the shit out of my shins."

Nolan: "The point being?"

Reese: "You figure it out."

Notes to myself, 06/19/68:

Bob Reese and I launched at 0300. I was leery about the three-quarters moon but it helped us approach the house thru the desert scrub without headlights. The old vet next door had a back-porch bug light but no lights on inside.

We parked about 200 yards shy and crept in. We were dressed in dark colors, wearing disposable gloves. No dogs barked. The only sign of life was a stray coyote that darted off at our approach.

Bob Reese held my penlight while I assessed the back door lock. A deadbolt. The knob's outside cylinder had been recently jimmied, fresh gouge marks in the brass. Still, it took me a sweaty two minutes to pop it.

The back door opened onto the kitchen. Once we were inside with the door closed, Reese squatted down and shined the penlight flat across the kitchen floor. Cockroaches scurried. Jeremiah McLemore's fanatical devotion to his truck's upkeep did not extend to his housekeeping. The kitchen floor looked like an archeological dig.

I squatted next to Reese. The penlight beam revealed boot tracks coming and going in bas relief. There was so much crud on the floor I was able to use my thumb as a measuring stick. The outgoing boot prints were slightly deeper. Bingo.

We ventured further in. I was careful to avoid the boot prints, not sure why. I wasn't conducting a forensic investigation; no one important would see the results of this illegal incursion. I just wanted to know what happened.

The rest of the kitchen floor and the carpeted living room had been trampled by the NPD as expected. Bob Reese turned to go back to his truck and monitor the scanner.

I snagged his arm. I wanted his eyeballs on the presumptive murder scene: JM's bedroom. Kitty corner to the living room, in front of the kitchen.

The bedroom was surprisingly well kept. No socks on the floor, closet and drawers closed. Framed watercolors of the desert on the wall, a black and white family photo on his dresser: Mom and Dad - a young JM and a toddler that he held close - in their Sunday best outside a stone church. They looked cold.

The bed had not been stripped. After making sure the blinds were closed tight I gave Reese the nod to use his much brighter Kel light. I got interested when his beam zeroed in on a spot of dried blood on a pillowcase. Not a big spot, but not a small one either.

Bob Reese shrugged it off. "Desert nosebleed."

"What's a desert nosebleed?"

"It comes from picking sand out of your dried-out schnozz."

I sent Reese off to lookout duty in his Bronco, then checked the phones in the bedroom and the kitchen for signs of a tap.

No luck, no surprise. An enemy contractor could be schooled in how to remove a tap after he topped off JM. A screwdriver and needle nose pliers is all you need.

It was time to go. My luck had held, I had evidence that bolstered my theory that JM had been murdered in his own bed by an enemy agent.

Things were going far too well.

I work in counterintelligence because my mentor, William King Harvey, put me there. The portly, bug-eyed Harvey was the first to cast doubt on the brilliant British double agent Harold 'Kim' Philby. He also had a successful run as Chief of Berlin Station in the mid-1950's. Bill Harvey has fallen on hard times since then because he was put in charge of Operation Mongoose, the Kennedy brothers' ill-fated attempt to assassinate Fidel Castro.

But that's a story for another time.

In any event Bill Harvey has a saying he likes to say. "Watch out you don't double cross yourself."

Harvey thought the CIA did that with Soviet defector Yuri Nosenko, a KGB captain who provided a trove of gold-plated intel which was rejected because Nosenko was considered to be part of a 'master plot' to penetrate the CIA.

What Harvey meant was to not jump to conclusions based on false assumptions. If Nosenko reported a KGB operation previously reported by another defector, Jim Angleton didn't count that in his favor because he assumed the KGB knew the operation had been compromised. If Nosenko reported a KGB operation not previously known, JJA judged the information doubtful because it couldn't be confirmed.

"Try talking your way out of that cage," said Harvey.

I quick stepped up to Reese's Ford Bronco. I had half a mind to slam the door loudly to see if anyone noticed. When you are sniffing around deep, dark strategic secrets someone is supposed to care.

We drove off. Bob Reese dropped me at my motel. I thanked him, gave him four one hundred dollar bills, and asked what his plans were for tomorrow.

Reese held up the bag of doggie downers he hadn't used.

"Think I'll make me some spaghetti and meatballs."

I'm pretty sure Bob Reese was joking but I couldn't swear to it.

Los Angeles Herald-Examiner

Friday, June 21, 1968   First edition

The Strange Death of Jeremiah McLemore

(by Maxwell J. Phillips, special to the Herald)

The Mojave Desert is a solemn place. Scientists say the area used to be home to grand lakes, lush vegetation and plumed wildlife. Then a volcano in the Woods Mountains erupted some twenty million years ago, raining down boulders and hot ash that killed every plant and animal within a radius of fifty miles.

Modern day Mojave hikers are heard to say, "We tread lightly here. This is one vast tomb."

That certainly proved true for 38-year-old Needles, California resident Jeremiah McLemore. His body, ravaged by coyotes, was discovered by Needles PD investigators on May 29th, in a remote area roughly ten miles north of Needles. The corpse lay just a few feet from his Jeep. The body was so disfigured that the San Bernardino County

Coroner's Office had to obtain dental records to make a positive identification.

Investigators found no immediate signs of foul play and the Coroner ruled the cause of death, "heat stroke precipitated by drug and alcohol intoxication." Not an unknown occurrence in this hardscrabble part of the country.

Jeremiah McLemore moved to Needles from his parent's modest home in Grand Island, Nebraska in 1963. He purchased a dump truck and established an independent trash hauling business that serviced local businesses and rural residents. He had recently acquired a large contract to haul refuse from a new addition to the area: Camp Harrison - also known as Camp X - a mysterious Army training camp directly across the Colorado River in Arizona.

And therein lies the rub. A highly-placed governmental source has told your humble reporter that McLemore was approached by a foreign intelligence agent who was eager to examine the trash removed from Camp Harrison, in order to discern the "true nature" of the activities taking place there.

My source did not know what cover story the foreign agent used to explain his interest in McLemore's trash hauls, but he indicated that Jeremiah became suspicious and contacted the Needles Police Department, though the NPD would not confirm this.

I am not privy to what takes place in Camp X. If I were I would not report it. However, as I have often been told by espionage officers over my long career, "We do not believe in coincidence."

Was Jeremiah McLemore's untimely death in the vast tomb of the Mojave a coincidence? Or were the strange circumstances of his death an elaborate cover for the assassination of an American citizen by foreign agents?

I don't know. That is for the authorities, and for you, to decide.

--Maxwell J. Phillips

via Telex

TE# 3744019-j

N₀ 53622

21 June 1968

TO: James J. Angleton, Chief of CI Staff,

            Clandestine Services, DDP

FROM: ROLLTOP

SUBJECT: Jeremiah McLemore

STATUS: **TOP SECRET**

CODING: TSJ-91

The Los Angeles Herald column by Max Phillips surprised me, especially his allegation that a foreign agent approached Jeremiah McLemore about the contents of his Camp X trash hauls. To my knowledge no one knew that McLemore had been contacted about his trash hauls but Officer Bell, myself and CI Staff via my cable to your office.

I took pains to sweat Ofc. Bell on this question. He assured me that he had not shared McLemore's confidence with his fellow officers. He only shared it with me when I informed him that his friend might be in grave danger.

I suppose it is possible that McLemore shared this information with a friend or neighbor, but to what end? From all accounts

McLemore was the silent type. And why would a friend or neighbor contact Maxwell Phillips?

From what I have gathered Max Phillips is a pompous ass, but I think we must take him at his word that he was contacted by a "highly-placed source." I assume you have not informed the NSA on this matter. That leaves only our own CI Staff.

Is that possible?

::TRANSMISSION COMPLETE::

via Telex   TE# 4972841-j

N₀ 53641

21 June 1968

TO: ROLLTOP

FROM: James J. Angleton, Chief of CI Staff,

            Clandestine Services, DDP

SUBJECT: Jeremiah McLemore

STATUS: **TOP SECRET**

CODING: TSJ-91

First, to answer your question; no, it is not possible that CI Staff
was the source for Mr. Phillip's risible newspaper article. I say
this with confidence because I did not permit distribution of the
transcript of your interview with Ofc. Bell. Of course the
recording was transcribed by the inimitable Miss K, my
steadfast amanuensis of twelve years and executor of my last
will and testament.

I believe you have overlooked an obvious source – our own
Directorate of Operations. Having cast doubt on a legion of
their supposed Soviet defectors over the years, our
counterparts view me as a modern day Torquemada casting
out heretics from my throne of gold. The message this leak to
Mr. Phillips sends to me is: "You see, we do have viable Soviet

sources with actionable intelligence. You are the apostate; it is we who are the true bearers of liturgical purity."

That the allegation Mr. Phillips reports is unsubstantiated would not trouble our counterparts at the Directorate of Operations unduly.

Consider this possibility: A simultaneous pas de deux between CIA Operations and KGB Special Service II, and our own CI department and KGB Operations.

Special Service II is using their 'defectors' to give CIA Operations disinformation that is then passed on to news outlets in an attempt to make us look inept, thus furthering SSII's objective of sowing distrust and discord between CIA Operations and CIA Counterintelligence.

Dastardly. But we are hardly ones to talk. A principal purpose of Camp X is to sow distrust and discord between KGB Ops and KGB SS II and, with any luck, Soviet Military Intelligence, GRU. In an ironic twist of fate, Maxwell Phillip's Soviet-sponsored newspaper article may serve to promote our objective.

Presumably SS II knows that none of its operatives approached J. McLemore. And, presumably, the same can be said of KGB Ops and the GRU. However, Phillip's article might set each one of these commissariats to actively wondering about the others.

Take note, good friend, you are a senior officer separated from his family on a lengthy posting, consigned to a dreary motel in the middle of nowhere. Our enemies may conclude that you have fallen out of favor. Be prepared for an approach; you know how to act insulted at this affront to your honor while leaving the door open a crack.

In the event of an overture it is imperative that we determine the affiliation of the agent, to discern whether he is KGB or GRU. The Phillip's article might prompt KGB's SSII to dispatch an agent because they suspect Camp X is an elaborate CI deception. If the agent is GRU, however, it would indicate the Red Army believes Camp X to be a legitimate weapons development outpost.

This will require you to take a photograph that we can conjugate against our various dossiers. I know that you generally disdain such gimmickry as the tie tack camera with which you have been equipped but, in this particular instance, I must insist.

::TRANSMISSION COMPLETE::

via Telex

TE# 4972841-j

N₀ 53677

21 June 1968

TO: James J. Angleton, Chief of CI Staff,

               Clandestine Services, DDP

FROM: ROLLTOP

SUBJECT: Jeremiah McLemore

STATUS: **TOP SECRET**

CODING: TSJ-91

Message received, if not completely comprehended. Will proceed as instructed with one caveat. Wearing a tie out here would make me look conspicuous since no one, save perhaps the local bank manager, does so. At least not in summertime.

If I can safely conduct a tail after contact – a difficult prospect in this small town of broad streets and wall to wall sunshine – I will take some snaps with my telephoto.

If that does not work, I will go to LA and employ a sketch artist.

::TRANSMISSION COMPLETE::

Notes to myself, 06/24/68:

Besides being an orchid breeder and a collector of fine French wines, Jim Angleton has a passion for fly fishing. Where he finds the time to pursue these hobbies I can't begin to tell you. But his characterization of me as "consigned to a dreary motel in the middle of nowhere", made it clear I was a tied and spindled fishing lure, bobbing just below the surface.

And a couple days later I did get a tug on the line, but not in the way I expected. What I expected was a note shoved under my door at night or someone slipping out of the shadows as I pretended to stumble home from The Rails - not someone knocking on my door at the crack of dawn.

"Lieutenant Nolan? Are you there?" said a young female.

I was puzzled. No foreign agent or emissary worth her salt would come calling at my domicile at this hour. It just wasn't done.

I checked the peephole, shook off the cobwebs and cracked open the door to an attractive young blonde with a California tan. She said she worked for Maxwell Phillips, the famous journalist, who very much wanted to talk to me. I said I wasn't interested.

"Mr. Phillips knows your real identity, Lieutenant."

This got my attention. She handed me a slip of paper.

"He will be at this telephone number until 9:45." She waved me a cheery goodbye and walked back down the stairs.

The KGB are very good at what they do. It was barely possible that this surfer girl was a clever ruse on their part. If Lt. Nolan was willing to talk to a famous journalist about his vocational frustrations, then perhaps Lt. Nolan was ripe for the plucking.

In any event, I needed to find out who was at the other end of the phone number. Jim Angleton would not be pleased to have me unmasked in a nationally syndicated newspaper column.

I drove to a pay phone I hadn't used before, roll of quarters in hand. I attached a mini mike to the back of the phone's hand-piece. Here is the transcript of our conversation:

"Maxwell Phillips."

"Lieutenant Dick Nolan. What do you want?"

"I'd like to speak with you about Jeremiah McLemore. My photogenic assistant Ginny is currently sitting in the parking lot of your motel in her candy apple red Camaro, waiting to whisk you north to my suite at the Sahara."

"Well, that answers one question."

"What's that?"

"You're not a spy posing as Maxwell Phillips."

"How so?"

"Your courier is a comely blonde in a red convertible who thumps on my door in front of God and everybody. She then sits in the parking lot and slathers herself with cocoa butter while waiting to chauffeur me up Highway 95 and down the Vegas Strip."

"I take it you think meeting in Vegas is a bad idea."

"Uh huh. Your column suggesting Jeremiah McLemore was assassinated by foreign agents means, I'm guessing, you are currently the fourth most-surveilled man on earth. Do you have a Plan B?"

"Well, let me see....tell Ginny we'll meet at the picnic spot instead. She'll know."

I drove back to the motel and told Ginny our meeting had been moved. She had no idea what the picnic spot referred to. We bounced it back and forth till the light dawned.

"Cottonwood Cove on Lake Mojave. Last summer, Max took me out on one of those 15-foot putt-putts you rent there, you know, trying to get something going. He brought along a blanket and a picnic basket. It was fucking hysterical."

No doubt. A rented motorboat cruising Lake Mojave would be reasonably secure from audio surveillance. I would carry my cigarette pack mini-recorder, so I couldn't very well ask Phillips to submit to a pat down search for a wire. We would have to do la danza de la muerte until we figured out how much we could trust each other.

I was surprised that Phillips had figured out my real identity. I was issued a uniform, a nameplate and a business card with the Army eagle on it that identified me as Lt. Richard Nolan. It had a phone number with a Pentagon exchange. If someone called, a secretary at Langley would answer; "Lt. Nolan's office."

The secretarial staff was given regular updates on my cover story in order to reassure anyone who inquired. They kept a log of such calls to alert me to somebody checking up on me. That was the extent of my backstopping.

I had never given Phillips my card of course. However, his interest in the strange death of Jeremiah McLemore meant he might have dispatched someone to photograph the Army Lt. riding around w. NPD cops; then try to match my photo to Knight-Ridder's file photos of known CIA personnel.

But so what? I had been very careful to avoid photographs since my old spy school file photo appeared on the front page of every newspaper in the country in 1948: a photo taken when I was a 19-year-old with a big Adam's apple.

I never went out in D.C. without a low-brimmed hat and sunglasses. The windows of our house were covered in reflective film and my car windows were smoked. On the rare occasions when friends and neighbors were invited over, they knew photos were verboten.

I didn't take these precautions in Needles because I didn't see the need. No one would have anything to compare them to. And, yes, I was dead tired of playing the anonymity game.

It was a puzzler. I would have to ask.

I politely declined Ginny's offer of a ride and followed her Camaro in my rental car, struggling to keep pace. We clocked the 65 miles to Cottonwood Cove in just under 49 minutes. That my Chevy's radiator didn't explode was a miracle. By the time we pulled into the gravel parking lot the Chevy Biscayne sounded like a fat man who had just climbed six flights of stairs.

We met Phillips at the boat dock. He was a fit man with a mahogany tan and a shock of white-blond hair under a broad-brimmed Panama hat. He looked a good deal older than his newspaper photo.

We left Ginny on the dock and cruised the blue Colorado in a 15-foot outboard. Phillips wore a pair of wraparound sunglasses and smoked a raggedy cheroot snugged into an ivory holder.

The transcript of our conversation, once the opening pleasantries were completed, is as follows. The marks of ellipses indicate gaps in the recording resulting from interference from the sputtering outboard motor.

(...) indicates a brief gap, (.....) indicates a longer one.

P: "You should know that I already have a column I can write; 'Why is Hal Schroeder, CIA counterintelligence honcho and legendary...posing as an Army Lieutenant and investigating the strange death of Jeremiah McLemore...the coroner ruled it accidental?'"

N: "How did you determine I was Hal Schroeder?"

P: "With a facial structure expert, assisted by a computer program. IBM has a program that takes a photo...20 or 30 years."

N: "Christ. It's a brave new world."

P: "And it's just getting started."

N: (inaudible)

P: "I don't generally expose legitimate federal undercover activity, Mr. Schroeder. But this leak, the one.....has the stink of office politics about it. It smells like a turf war."

N: "Between who and who?"

P: "Who and whom and I can't say."

N: "Can't say or don't know?"

P: "I can't say because I don't know. But my.....I'm being hosed."

N: "Then why publish that piece about McLemore?"

P: "I had an official source."

N: "In your article you said it was a highly-placed governmental source but...which government. You care to be..."

P: "I don't use Communist officials as confidential sources, Mr. Schroeder."

N: "Glad to hear it, Mr. Phillips."

P: "And it was a column not an article."

N: "Excuse me all to.....ever knows the ultimate source of a leak. Could be anybody, could be..."

(At this point the sputtering outboard mercifully found its rhythm and settled down.)

P: "One of those orphaned Soviet Bloc defectors who keep showing up on the front steps of Langley till Jim Angleton chases them off with a wet broom?"

N: "Was the original source a Soviet defector?"

P: "No, of course not."

N: "How can you be sure?"

P: "Because my official source was not a glad-handing salesman from the CIA Directorate of Operations but a glum bank examiner like yourself."

N: "Someone on the CI staff? Who?"

P: "I will rule out only one possibility for you, Mr. Schroeder, and that's your boss."

N: "Angleton?"

P: "I never trust a source who's about to be sacked, too many scores to settle."

N: "Angleton's on thin ice?"

P: "Old news. The President asked for his assessment of the Viet Cong's Tet offensive. The Scarecrow thought it would be modest."

N: "So did most of the DoD."

P: "The difference is that Angleton has anointed himself as the knower of all truth. And there's more. One of the Soviet defectors Angleton nixed as a plant was deported to Moscow last week, and summarily executed."

N: "Christ, how do you get this stuff?!"

P: "As a hired hand, you learn only what the boss man wants you to. As a journalist, I learn what he wants to keep secret."

N: "Sure. Fed to you by his rivals and enemies."

P: "And that's where you, an Angleton loyalist I presume, come in. I would like to hear your take on the strange death of Jeremiah McLemore.'

N: "The FBI's investigating. Why not wait for their report?"

P: "I'm not a beat reporter, Mr. Schroeder."

N: "You want a scoop."

P: "Of course."

Could I tell Phillips what the boys and I had discovered at JM's death scene even though Angleton had dismissed it?

I had to give him something. If I corroborated Phillips' murder-by-a-foreign-agent theory, what was the harm? JJA himself said that Phillips' article might further his objective by sowing doubt between rival Soviet agencies.

But I'd be entrusting my career to a man who wrote tell-all articles for Playboy magazine. A thought occurred.

N: "I can get you everything you need to know about McLemore from a Needles cop who was his best friend and the first to discover and investigate the death; but you have to leave me out of the story. Completely out of the story."

P: "Why would I do that?"

N: "Because this young cop's a reporter's wet dream, a regular quote machine. And he won't agree to an interview unless I give him the nod."

P: "All right. I'll agree to your conditions with one stipulation: I want an interview with this young man within 24 hours."

N: "He's working graves. Give me 36."

P: "As you say."

We cruised up Lake Mojave - which is not really a lake but just a wider part of the Colorado River - in companionable silence.

P: "Beautiful country, isn't it?"

N: "I've taken quite a liking to it, not sure why."

P: "Care to hear an old man's thoughts on the matter?"

N: "Sure."

P: "As a spy who has spent his career hiding behind phone poles in dark alleys, and doing the metaphorical equivalent in the halls and warrens of the CIA, you appreciate the Mojave sunshine."

N: "There might be something to that."

P: "Indeed. So, Mr. Schroeder, what the fuck is going on at Camp X?"

N: "I wouldn't tell you if I did, but the truth is I don't."

P: "What?"

N: "Know."

P: "Why not?"

N: "I've been demoted to a field agent for this operation, Phillips, I'm vulnerable to kidnap and interrogation. They don't trust us with the big picture stuff."

P: "I find that hard to believe."

N: "Which part?"

P: "All of it."

N: "Welcome to the club."

We laughed, then boated up the river for a time, swung around and headed back to the dock.

P: "Who are the top three?"

N: "Sorry?"

P: "You said I figured to be the fourth most-surveilled man on earth. Who are the top three?"

N: "Off the record?"

P: "Off the record."

The remainder of this recording is inaudible due to a sudden surge of passing speedboats. I have reconstructed the remaining dialogue from memory:

N: "Two of the top three change all the time, and they're not the major political figures you'd expect because movements of Presidents and Prime Ministers are well publicized, and their communication security is airtight. But there is one world leader whose security apparatus is bloody awful. Soviet Bloc agencies routinely penetrate it to glean intel shared within the Western World."

P: "And who is this world leader?"

H: "Think about it. What world leader doesn't give a hang about state secrets?"

P: "I'm good at asking questions, Mr. Schroeder, not so good at answering them. Give me a hint."

H: "Dominus vobiscum."

P: "Ah, of course. The Pope."

After we docked I exchanged contact info with Phillips, tipped my cap to Ginny and headed south at a speed well within the posted limit. I needed to conserve my eighth of a tank.

I knew there was a Sunoco station about fifty miles south, just above Needles. I could have turned north and found a nearer station on the road to Vegas, but we Teutonic-types don't do detours. We hew to the most direct route between point A and point B and devil take the hindmost. Stupid no doubt, considering it was one hundred and five degrees or thereabouts, but I wasn't about to change now.

I turned off the AC and rolled down the windows. When the fuel gauge sank below E, I rolled up the windows to reduce drag and used my index finger to windshield wiper the sweat off my eyelids.

Fifteen minutes later I crawled into the Sunoco station with three teaspoons of petrol to spare. I parked, peeled the back of my shirt off the driver's seat, scared up two dimes for the vending machine and glugged down two cold bottles of Coca Cola.

I knew the story of Bell contaminating a potential crime scene would get him in trouble with the Chief of Police, but he'd already told me he had one foot out the door. I wasn't surprised at his reply to my suggestion that he agree to be interviewed by Phillips.

I didn't record it, but I remember it distinctly.

B: "I'm in. I could use the publicity. If the Chief cans me it's even better."

N: "How do you figure?"

B: "'Rookie officer defies top cop to find friend's killer.' Something like that, Phillips will know how to work it."

Two days later Phillips wrote a column detailing the discovery and investigation of JM's death scene by Bell, Clovis and William Redfeather of the Paiute Nation. My name was not mentioned. Other than that, the account was accurate.

Phillips knew his trade. He brought the scene to life with vivid detail and concluded with a blockbuster question:

"My previous column quoted an anonymous federal official who strongly suggested that McLemore had been assassinated by an intelligence operative from the Soviet Bloc. My subsequent investigation has uncovered no evidence or indication of that. Could there be an even more sinister explanation of the strange death of Jeremiah McLemore?"

Hoo boy. Jim Angleton was going to love that.

My dearest husband,

I don't want to know the details of your work, but I sense from our phone call that you are troubled and doubtful about what you have been sent out to the desert to do. Please do not dismiss this with a regal wave of your hand. A wife knows these things.

The less said about our beloved Helen, the better. She is, by turns, weepy and defiant, a Coleen to her bones. But do not concern yourself, she will be fine.

I console myself most nights with a glass of our favorite white Bordeaux while old Mrs. Harrigan stumbles and clatters about in the kitchen. My offers of help are met with scowls. I understand that we must employ domestic help who have been properly approved. My only complaint is that the proper approval process takes so bloody long that the help needs my help to climb the steps!

Our superb record collection is my close companion...

If I invite/ a boy some night/ to enjoy my fine finnan haddie/I just adore/ his asking for more/ but my heart belongs to Daddy.

Everyone loves the steamy Marilyn Monroe movie version of this song but I do so much prefer Ella Fitzgerald's recording. So silky and carefree. And after the 20th or so listening it dawned on me - I do believe the lady in question was inviting the boy to enjoy something other than smoked haddock!

I am so naïve. And pampered to be able to write this letter on vellum stationary from a comfy couch.

And so lonely.

Your loving wife,

L

My darling girl,

I am writing you a letter that begs to be written but one I will never post because I know it would make you sad.

Your last letter broke my heart. I hate to think of you sunk in our cold, white, over-upholstered living room with a stack of LP's on the record player and a bottle of wine on ice to console you. I know the other wives have been cool to you — a poor girl from the Old Country, bored by bridge games and country club gossip.

Truth is they are envious: Of your blazing eyes and wicked wit. Of your lusty laugh. Of your dimples.

I could go on.

My Catholic guilt is eating me alive. I have abandoned my family in their time of need. I swear I would not blame you if you had an affair to soothe your loneliness. I would not!

But know that I am living a monkish life in this one-horse town where, admittedly, the temptations are slim. All right. None.

I love you Lilly. You will never know how much.

Notes to myself, 06/29/68:

(None of the dialogue below was recorded, no same day notes were made. This is what was said to the best of my next-day recollection.)

Bell and I met at The Rails Saturday evening, just after sundown. He was keen to tell me about his interview w. Max Phillips, which he thought went well.

Not long after we parked ourselves at the bar I noticed, in the wall mirror, two shaggy-haired young men enter with fishing gear, rods and reels covered in dark tarps with red logos - a couple tourists slaking their thirst after a day on the river.

After they seated themselves at a table behind us, I noticed the tip of one of their fishing rods was tilted in our direction. I asked Bell a question...

Nolan: "Is fishing easy here, like a trout farm where the fish all but jump in the boat?"

Bell: "Hell no."

Nolan: "So the appeal is spending a lazy day in the hot sun drinking cold beer."

Bell: "Yeah. It's called fishing."

Nolan: "Do fishermen wear clothing to protect them from the sun?"

Bell: "Hat and a shirt in the summertime."

Nolan: "Long sleeve shirts?"

Bell: "Never seen that."

I gestured toward the newcomers.

Nolan: "Then why are their forearms mayonnaise white?"

Bell: "Maybe they just rolled into town."

Nolan: "Then why bring the gear in? You might do that after fishing if you were afraid it would get stolen out of your truck. But if you've just rolled into town, you'd stash your gear in your room before venturing out."

Bell considered this, stood up and walked over to the men. I followed. They reeked of pot. Bell flashed his badge and asked to see their fishing licenses.

The older of the two said, "That's not a Fish & Game badge."

Bell was quick. "Due to a staffing shortage, the Dept. of Fish & Game has deputized the NPD to perform their enforcement functions within the city limits."

The men had no fishing licenses.

Bell: "Then I'm afraid I'll have to confiscate your fishing poles. Once you obtain a license you can reclaim them at the station."

The younger of the two looked nervous but the older one stared daggers. I didn't want trouble, I wanted an NRF operation. No records filed.

These twerps obviously weren't seasoned contractors of the KGB or the GRU; they were hired help. Hired by whom was the question.

I put a restraining hand on Bell's arm. "Let these gents enjoy their vacation, I'm sure they'll get their fishing licenses first thing tomorrow."

The twerps promised to do so. I continued.

"St. Croix reels. Nice, heard good things about them. Mind if I take a look?"

All eyes in the bar were now upon us. Bell cocked his head at Big Ray, who moved to block the front door, all bad blood forgotten.

The older guy – he was all of 30 - mumbled, "Suit yourself."

What followed was one of the more ludicrous encounters of my long career. I unzipped the tarp to find a long skinny mike taped to the top of the fishing pole. "What's this?"

The older guy sighed. "It's a directional mike."

"For finding fish," added the younger guy, quickly.

"How does that work?" asked Bell.

"Well, when you lay your rod over the surface of the water you can hear them."

"The fish?"

"Yeah."

"Doing what?" said Bell.

"Umm, you know. Swimming."

"My goodness gracious, what will they think of next?"

114

Bell said it so convincingly that, for a moment, I thought he was serious.

I got to the point. "Who are you boys working for?"

The boys didn't answer. I continued.

Nolan: "Unauthorized recording of a private conversation is a crime in the state of California. Isn't that right, officer?"

Bell: "A felony, punishable by up to ten years in prison."

OlderGuy: "Hey, look, we're Foley artists, we record movie dialogue. A guy offered us a thousand cash to tape some conversations. He put us up in a motel down the road and said wait for his call."

Bell: "And then what?"

OG: "He called, described you two and gave this address."

Bell: "And that didn't sound hinky to you?"

OG: "There's a SAG strike on, work's been slow."

Nolan: "What's this guy's name?"

OG: "Wendell. Didn't give a last name."

Bell: "Wendell No-Last-Name just waltzed into your office and offered you a grand to commit a felony?"

YoungerG: "No, no. There's a dive bar in North Hollywood where film crews hang."

OlderG: "He got us plotzed."

Nolan: "This Wendell, did he have any sort of foreign accent?"

OG: "I dunno. Polish?"

This got me to wondering. The suspicious stranger who contacted JM gave his name as Wendell. But why would he use the same alias? And why trust these twerps to conduct your surveillance?

Seemed like someone was trying to convince me that Wendell really existed. Not sure why but I had an inkling.

I asked for a description of Wendell. "Tall, heavyset, mid-40's, used a lot of Brylcreem."

I asked for the time and location of the exchange of the money for the recording. Bell promised no arrests if they cooperated.

The Foley artists said the meet was set for one a.m. at their motel, The 66. I asked them if their room was upstairs or down.

Upstairs. Good. We wouldn't have to cover the back window.

I told them to stay put. If anyone was keeping watch outside, it would look like they were still on the job.

I told Bell to call Bob Reese and ask him to grab a first-floor room at the 66 Motel as an observation post - then come pick us up a block away after we left by the back door at midnight. That would give us time to set up a stakeout.

I gave Big Ray ten bucks to babysit the fishermen till 12:45, then walk them out to their car. Ray palmed the sawbuck and nodded like we did this all the time.

The Foley artists could have lit out for LA at 12:45, of course, but they were so plotzed I was more concerned they wouldn't make it the four blocks to their motel for the 1 a.m. exchange.

But they made it with five minutes to spare.

I was hiding in the bed of a pickup in the parking lot w. my infrared camera as Bell peered thru the curtains in the downstairs room Bob Reese had booked.

The Foley artists stumbled up the stairs to their room and closed the door.

Bell and I waited a long time. Wendell never showed.

(There was no date noted on this document. – *ed.*)

Note to the reader:

I have kept this log as a means to document a very strange assignment, and to maintain what little sanity I have left. I will pass it along to my daughter Helen on some distant day. It occurred to me that she, and by extension you, dear reader, should Helen choose to share this, would need to know what the hell it is that I do at CIA.

I am what they call a Reports Officer. When one of my Case Officers in the field gathers intel from a source he cables it on to me. I evaluate it for credibility and importance and recommend to JJA who to forward it to: State, the FBI or NSA.

If it's critical, the Director of Central Intelligence will include it in the President's Daily Brief.

It's an important job, more so than my former job as an overseas Case Officer. It is also mind-numbing.

I was good at recruiting foreign field agents but lousy at learning languages. I grew up with Deutsche and managed to learn dumbbell Spanish, but a good case officer needs to be fluent in half a dozen tongues. The Agency doesn't let you linger for long in one country because, over time, the enemy sniffs you out.

So Jim Angleton kicked me upstairs. It was a swell move on his part and I bent to my new job with all the enthusiasm I could muster. 'Bent' being the operative word. I sat at a desk poring over stacks of CO reports, the volume growing year by year. After almost a decade I needed a break and said so.

It wasn't just the workload. After ten years of evaluating reports in a windowless room, lucky to get home to Falls Church by 7:00 most nights, I felt like a stranger to myself. I was thrilled when Angleton sent me off to do some fieldwork in the Mojave Desert.

I should have been suspicious on two counts: Why send a middle-aged desk jockey off to do rigorous fieldwork in an inhospitable place he'd never been? And why not give said desk jockey an in-depth briefing about Camp X, the citadel he was being sent to protect?

I ignored those clanging sentry bells for no other reason than I wanted to. As Winston Churchill supposedly said, "No one asks hard questions of good fortune."

Lilly said she was happy for me but I knew she was worried. As it stood we had weekends together and I was home every night.

My wife had traveled with me to my foreign postings in Panama City and Budapest when Helen was little, but it was different now with a daughter in high school and a domestic routine. We had put down roots, if a spy can do such a thing.

So why was Lilly so concerned?

Well, she had never warmed to Jim Angleton despite his purring charm. She thought him unbalanced and paranoid and getting worse. And I was to report directly to him on this special assignment.

I do think JJA has a bit of a Christ complex but Lilly has a different take. She rarely got to see Angleton's quicksilver mind in action; never got to challenge him as I did about some jarring statement, and watch him parry my questions for the better part of an hour with obscure references that only he knew.

Lilly stood back from all that and gave me her assessment: James Jesus Angleton was a wayward saint in search of martyrdom.

Whew.

For some reason, I couldn't resist rising to his defense.

Charm can be a powerful weapon: Kim Philby used his posh British gent act to deflect suspicion for decades. But Jim Angleton's appeal was different – more abstract, poetic.

On the subject of charm, for instance, he would say, "An accomplished CI officer does not charm the birds from the trees, in the popular locution. That is not useful. Anyone can dislodge birds from a tree. What an accomplished CI officer does is charm the snakes from the ground."

On the question of how I kept this journal secret for so many years, the answer is straightforward: There are many methods for securing documents when you are on the road - sending them in a registered letter addressed to a designated PO Box - capturing them on a roll of microfilm you conceal in a tooth cavity - using microdots or invisible ink to embed them in a book or magazine.

All well and good, but susceptible to screw-ups and faulty execution.

In clandestine activity, as in most things other than counterintelligence, the simpler the better. I didn't attempt to code my writings; anyone interested enough to steal them would have the intellectual firepower to decode them in short order. And the fact that my writing was not in code would confuse the crap out of the KGB.

So here is Hal Schroeder's foolproof personal method of document concealment: Write the doc as soon as possible to capture details. Then proceed directly to the bank and deposit said pages in your safe deposit box; the one where they check your signature and the bankers have a matching key.

If you are past bankers' hours, sleep with the docs under your mattress and a handgun under your pillow.

It's worked for me.

Notes to myself, 07/01/68:

I drove to 29 Palms to cable James Angleton about our soiree with the Foley artists.

I laid out the facts, but not my conclusions. It was the first time I had deliberately misled the man who had kept my family in beans and bacon all these years. It gave me a very queasy feeling.

I prepared to cool my heels for the standard 60 minutes to await a reply from Angleton, but the teletype clattered to life just a few minutes later. The first part of his reply made it official: Jim Angleton and Hal Schroeder were now lying to one another.

I wasn't sure what to make of the second part, however. (See cable #53801.)

via Telex

No 53801

1 July, 1968

TO:	ROLLTOP
FROM:	James J. Angleton, Chief of CI Staff,
	Clandestine Services, DDP
SUBJECT:	Jeremiah McLemore
STATUS:	**TOP SECRET**
CODING:	TSJ-91

A timely report. Wendell rears his ugly head once more. That he did not arrive to collect the recorded material at the end of the evening suggests he knew the trap was set, perhaps when you and the officer left by the back door.

A chance missed, but I sympathize. As you have mentioned, the open terrain makes covert action ne'er to impossible.

Change of subject:

New developments have caused me to reassess our preliminary conclusion that Jeremiah McLemore was not a Soviet collaborator. Said developments have me inclined to believe he was in full collusion.

I will explain anon. Suffice it to say that you should expect the unexpected.

::TRANSMISSION COMPLETE::

Notes to myself, 07/01/68:

Jeremiah McLemore was in full collusion w. the enemy?
That didn't square w. any evidence I'd seen. It made me
wonder what source JJA had that I did not.

With a blind eye assist from the NPD I had been able to
connive enough personal data – bank statements,
telephone bills and the like – to create a credible portrait
of Jeremiah McLemore as he lived and breathed in
Needles, CA.

Dull reading, JM lived a quiet life.

Or had I missed something?

This letter was decoded by Hal Schroeder upon receipt, which is why it is presented in his hand. The exact date of receipt is not known but Hal makes reference to it in his notes that follow. – *ed.*

My dearest husband,

It took me 4ever to write this letter. Writing in code reminds me of poetry. U say one thing and mean another.

I so enjoyed your last, the one about the lady in the pancakes, but it seemed late. I checked postmark, airmailed over a wk ago.

And your signature, your tiny brow clipping sealed in the flap, was missing.

I was bad. I did not look 4 your signature b4 removing letter. I was 2 eager to hear your voice! (And flap was intact, gave a good rip.)

I searched. Sofa, coffee table, carpet on hands and knees. No signature. Was letter steamed?

I know better than to call, this is why I write in code.

Should I be afraid?

Should we?

Your loving wife,

L

Notes to myself, 07/02/68:

I decided to put Camp X under observation even though I knew I would get my tit in a wringer if Jim Angleton found out. I did this because of something Angleton didn't do. He didn't ask me to find a new trash hauler to replace Jeremiah McLemore.

If covertly disposing of Camp X's refuse was so all-fired important, as the previous elaborate dumping regimen involving abandoned mines suggested, why not? It was possible Camp Commander Washburn had made separate arrangements – somebody had to collect the trash – but I should have been informed.

I didn't know what really went on inside that gray steel building because I wasn't need-to-know. I was now. When they start steaming open your letters home it's time to find out what the hell is going on.

'They' didn't figure to be the KGB. They'd know I wouldn't be clumsy enough to reveal Camp X secrets to my wife and put her in jeopardy. It smelled like a turf war, as Maxwell Phillips said.

Intramural spying among confederate agencies is verboten, but it goes on a lot more than you'd think. That is, it goes on a lot more than you'd think if you're a dewy-eyed resident of Happy Valley. Most likely suspect – J. Edgar Hoover. I'll explain later.

Bright and early on Monday, June 24th, I drove northeast on Harbor Street, crossed the river and headed toward Camp X. I wasn't followed.

The camp sat on a brown patch of dirt and was flanked by a ridge of mountains about half a mile to the east; a good vantage point if you had a high-powered telescope but too distant for binoculars. A craggy mesa about two hundred yards south of the camp was the only nearby high ground within binoc range.

I lusted after JM's 4-wheel Willys as my rented Chevy bucked and swayed through the off-road terrain, coarse and rocky one minute, soft and silty the next.

When I was out of sight of the main road I parked the exhausted Biscayne and hoofed it, wearing my bushman's wide-brimmed hat, my shoulder-slung canteen, my long sleeve khaki shirt and matching shorts and my new knee socks and hiking boots. The helpful salesclerk at Claypool's bagged his weekly quota when I walked in. He also sold me a state-of-the-art compass because "the magnetic pull of the Cinder Mountains makes the average compass go kerflooey."

If I had to cite one example of why the free enterprise American economic system is superior to that of the Soviets, I would nominate Claypool's Department Store, in Needles, California.

I slogged up to the top of the craggy butte dotted with Joshua trees and searched for signs that it had been used as a surveillance post. All I found was a fire pit and half-a-dozen empty bottles of Ripple. I found a low ridge of rocks and spent a few minutes digging myself a suitable hidey-hole with my latrine entrenching tool. Then I settled in to watch and wait.

And sweat my brains out.

The forecast was for a high of 112. The heat didn't seem to bother the fire ants and lizards who kept me company but I was woozy in half an hour, the exposed flesh of my knees and thighs an angry red. I didn't buy the shiny thermal reflector blanket I saw at Claypool's because it would have advertised my presence to low-flying aircraft.

This turned out to be a good decision because a helicopter swooped in from the northwest and landed near the front gate shortly before one. A commercial chopper but not a Bell-47. It was a big bird, somewhere between a Cobra and a Huey. Its rotor wash didn't kick up much dust, which told me it landed on this spot frequently.

The gate guard, who was perched in a steel and glass box outside the ten-foot tall corrugated black steel gate, said something into a phone, then jumped out to meet the chopper. About thirty seconds later the front gate broke in two and swung outwards, as if to repel invaders.

It looked as if the gate guard had no way of opening the gate from outside. He had to call in a request. Poor schmuck was on his own if the Mongol hordes descended.

The walls that surrounded the compound were poured concrete, painted brown and topped with coils of concertina wire, steel-shrouded cameras on every corner.

Two men in shades and dark green jumpsuits jumped out of the helicopter. Another man in similar attire handed them what looked like strongboxes from the baggage compartment. There wasn't so much as a hand truck to ease their load, so the men carried two strongboxes apiece into the compound, waved in by an M16-toting uniformed guard. I couldn't make out which service uniform he was wearing.

Scant minutes later the uniformed guard escorted the two men back to the chopper, which swooped off in a fat hurry, heading east this time.

Well. What was that all about?

One of the most persistent rumors swirling around Camp X was that it was a front for chemical or biological weapons research. Scratch bio off the list. The delivery boys weren't wearing hazmat suits, and the strongboxes were hand-carried into the compound. Not something you'd do with deadly anthrax samples.

Dangerous chemicals? I didn't know. But unless the chemicals had a nuclear half-life ticking away, why not slip them in by truck in the dead of night and avoid the big production?

I was suffering from heat prostration maybe, speculating based on a few crumbs of intel and trying to convince myself it was okay to punk out now, go home and take a cold shower. I did the next best thing. I doffed my hat, poured a glug of water on my head and shivered in the heat.

I maintained vigilance best I could, popped a salt pill, nipped at my canteen and thought of my wife and daughter, a luxury I didn't have in my stakeouts behind German lines. That soothed my fevered brow for about thirty seconds.

I drizzled water on my burning knees. I made notes in my notebook. I slowed my breathing and stretched out my spine. I found a smooth patch of dirt and laid on my back, watched a hawk cruising on thermals high above.

I rolled over like a rotisserie chicken and laid on my front. I noticed a faint aroma that seemed familiar.

Experts say smell has the strongest connection to memory of all the senses, which seems right to me. I was drowsing in a long checkout line at a grocery store a few years ago when I got a strong whiff of Lilly's perfume. I instinctively spun around to kiss her, and scared the bejesus out of the lady behind me.

I let my mind wander down memory lane, it didn't have anything else to do. I had already counted the number of hairs below my knuckles on the fingers and thumbs of both hands. Quick – which digits, (a) have the most hairs and, (b) the least hairs below the knuckles? No peeking.

(a) ring fingers and, (b) thumbs. Stakeouts tend to do this to you.

I lay there some more. My mind refused to wander at 112 degrees.

I sat up and drizzled more water on my noggin. The water dripping past my nose sparked a memory - Christmas dinner in Cleveland decades ago. My mother always prepared the traditional German feast. That was the faint, nostalgic aroma I recognized. What I smelled like was a cooking goose. Quite appropriate under the circumstances.

I was just that close to nutsville when I heard a diesel whine in the far distance.

I grabbed my binocs. A shiny blue and silver motor coach was approaching from the north, the kind they use to haul sightseers to the Hoover dam. It looked like an eight-wheeled hallucination as it plowed through the heat waves rising from the asphalt. Was Camp X a vacation destination now? Did they give guided tours and charge admission?

Those were the questions posed by my parboiled brain. As it turned out I wasn't that far afield.

The front gates swung wide as the bus pulled up. The M16-toting guard and a graying man dressed in a cream-colored linen suit hurried out to greet them. I had only met Camp Commander Joseph Washburn once, but he was a no-nonsense colonel who wouldn't be caught dead in a cream-colored suit. The man in the linen did look a bit like Maxwell Phillips, but of course that was impossible.

I put down my binoculars.

Ice chest, Harold. The next time you conduct surveillance in the Mojave Desert, bring along an ice chest. Fill it with those blue ice packs you chill in the freezer overnight. I hadn't done that because I didn't want to haul the extra weight and, besides, I had a canteen of frosty water slung over my shoulder. A canteen whose canvas cover I had soaked in water for evaporative cooling. A canteen whose contents by one o'clock in the afternoon could readily poach an egg.

I watched intently to see who exited from this motor coach with the smoked windows. The bus had parked at an angle that made seeing the disembarking passengers difficult. I did catch glimpses as they were escorted inside the massive gates.

They were a small, slow-moving group, middle aged and up. Men in dark suits ill-suited to the blazing heat; a few in more casual attire appeared to be toting young women who were not their wives.

For anyone reading this who is wondering why I was not snapping pix with a telephoto lens, let me remind you that unauthorized photo reconnaissance of a secret facility is a federal crime. Bad enough I kept this journal.

I needed to endure the insufferable heat for another hour. The young women in attendance got my attention. They made me suspect this might be a side trip on an Agency-funded Congressional junket to Vegas. If so the heavy-hitters would expect to be wined and dined for making the long trek to the middle of nowhere. If they were on a legitimate fact-finding tour, however, and the young women were administrative staff, well, the group would be back on the bus fairly soon.

I spent a miserable hour hunting shade from the volcanic rocks as the sun shifted. I sipped hot water and gnawed on my salami and Swiss cheese sandwich. Searing heat is not all bad. The bread was toasted, the Swiss cheese melted, and the fire ants added a nice crunch.

When I started back down to my Chevy, the blue and silver motor coach was still in place.

The following morning, in the bathroom mirror, I saw scalded red rings around both my eyes. Turns out binoculars get hot in the Mojave Desert in the summertime.

Notes to myself, 07/03/68:

Based on what I observed yesterday I have come to believe
that Camp X is a front for a front. What I mean by that is
that everyone suspects that it's not really an Army
training camp, but a front for a more covert activity: a
chemical or bio weapons' development lab, an
interrogation vault for Soviet Bloc defectors, perhaps a
processing depot for sigint (signal intelligence) data sent
down from satellites.

But I didn't see signs of any of that. What I suspect is that
the gray steel building is a propaganda podium for Jim
Angleton's CI Staff. An isolated, well-upholstered spot to
massage D.C. decision makers thru slick presentations
detailing intrepid overseas sleuthing and charts of
suspected mole networks inside allied govt's, punctuated
by generous servings of barrel-aged Kentucky bourbon,
prime Texas sirloin and God knows what else.

The ten-foot corrugated steel gates, the concertina wire,
and the clusters of antennas on the roof were window
dressing, designed to make the KGB, much like Officer Bell
and the locals, speculate themselves into a coma.

Jim Angleton has a favored quote: "The essence of
disinformation isn't lying, it's provocation."

Which raised the question - what was his disinformation
trying to provoke?

Angleton is an expert on orchid breeding. Seems orchids
are masters of disinformation, tricking insects into
pollinating their flowers. He was fond of one in particular,
the Tricerus or somesuch. This orchid has on its flower a

three-dimensional replica of the genitalia of a female fly, right down to the microscopic hairs. This prompts male flies to buzz in, do their business, then carry the orchid pollen to the next flower.

In this man's opinion, that is what that latticework of antennas atop the gray steel box at the center of Camp X was equivalent to for Soviet spy satellites flying overhead: microscopic fly genitalia.

But I've been wrong before. In point of fact, I'm an ace at making an ass out of u & me.

When I was a case officer in Budapest prior to the Hungarian Revolution in '56, I had a double I was running by the name of Lajos. He worked for the Hungarian Ministry of Home Affairs and was giving me so much of what I wanted to know that I became suspicious.

I tailed him after hours for a week. He met twice with a certain young lady in dark, out-of-the-way places where they had intense, hushed conversations in which she did most of the talking. They didn't kiss or nuzzle, it wasn't an assignation. And when she darted away, he would write furiously in a notepad.

I was able to identify the young woman as a low-ranking Communist official; Christian name, Mara. Since Lajos had never mentioned her, I assumed she was dictating party-approved disinformation to Lajos to pass on to me.

When you suspect a source of double dealing, you are not supposed to confront them directly so as not to tip your hand. That is why I offhandedly mentioned to Lajos that a young lady by the name of Mara was suspected of peddling worthless Hungarian gov't chickenfeed to Western agencies, and did he know her by any chance?

No, he did not.

Lajos should have told me that he did know Mara, that they had grown up together as neighbors. It would have saved her life.

But Lajos didn't do that. I suppose he thought he was protecting her anonymity. As if there was any such thing in Communist Hungary.

I continued to run Lajos for a bit. Disinformation is valuable because it tells you what the enemy wants you to believe. You can turn it on its head and believe the opposite, what we call a mirror read.

But like many who cross over, Lajos was a psychological car wreck. When I could no longer tolerate his hysterics, I cut the cord and sent him packing. Literally.

Come to learn years later that Mara feared she was about to be purged by the State Security Police because her clandestine lover was an anti-gov't rabble rouser.

Mara's parents and younger brother had fled to the U.S. before the Iron Curtain descended. She wanted to share news about her life and some treasured childhood memories in hopes Lajos could pass them along to her family.

She knew what was coming, she knew Lajos was going to flee b4 he knew.

"Yet she never asked me to help her, never asked to come along," he said in a letter I received in 1962.

Lajos managed to escape to Spain before Soviet tanks rolled into Budapest on that bloody November day. As it turns out I did him a favor by showing him the door. His letter told me all about Mara and how much he missed her. And he thanked me profoundly, as if I had purposefully frog marched him out of Hungary just in time.

Lagos' letter made me feel like shit. Had I not made a false assumption about their relationship, I could have smuggled Mara to freedom. She was tried as a traitor to the People's Republic and executed in 1957.

In those days, the Hungarian Party was known for a more compassionate brand of Communism than some of the other Soviet satellites. They didn't shoot or hang female traitors for instance. I have no idea how they killed Mara. But she was a beautiful young woman; the ÁVH would have had their fun with her.

And I have tried my damndest to avoid jumping to false conclusions ever since.

The Tribal Times

Vol. 117   *July 21, 1973*

"The Wisdom of the Fire Ant"

-- by William Redfeather

I made my bones as a Paiute tracker in 1968. The local cops in Needles and beyond thought I had super-Injun tracking powers and I milked that for all it was worth till I settled down and got a real job. In a funny way, the pigs were right.

A couple space cadets from San Francisco camped their VW bus down by the Colorado River in February of 1968. Their five-year-old son did not respond to their calls at sunset. They called the Needles PD an hour later. The NPD called me a couple hours after that.

Legend has it that I shushed all the coppers, bent down, zoned in and heard the boy's whimpers from a mile away.

Truth is I didn't hear crap. I had been in a rock band since I was sixteen and was half deaf. What I did was question the parents. What had the boy seen that had sparked his interest as they drove toward the campsite?

A five-year-old in a strange place doesn't wander so far off that he can't be called at dinnertime. Not unless he has a destination in mind.

But the stoner parents couldn't answer my question. I knew that they had driven in from the north, so I put on my five-year-old hat. What had I seen from the car that I would want to go explore?

The scary, beautiful black and red Cinder Domes! They were many miles away, but a five-year-old wouldn't know that. That gave our search party a general direction. Northwest.

But northwest covered a lot of dirt.

It was bughouse cold that February night, the rattlesnakes and coyotes would be hunkered in their holes and burrows. The young boy – his name was Sunrise, I shit you not - was safe from those predators. But there was another nocturnal predator on the hunt that night, one with a better network.

Fire ants will eat just about anything, but meat is their bell-ringer. They are aggressive little suckers who sting their prey in concert. Their venom can cause anaphylactic shock. It would not be beyond them to kill and consume a five-year-old boy.

Forager ants are the bloodhounds of the colony. Their super-intense olfactory sense directs them to food sources like carrion. Or about-to-be carrion. They communicate telepathically with the nest when they make a find.

It's true, I swear!

I used my flashlight to search for them, marching forager ants. I crisscrossed back and forth as we advanced and it didn't take me ten minutes to find several within twenty yards of one another, all marching in the same direction in their steady and relentless way.

The cops thought I was looking for footprints.

Once I knew the precise bearing to follow it was pretty easy. We found little Sunrise curled up against a rock, shivering and crying into his knees. The jumping chollas had stuck his arms and legs with cactus spines so I did my best to clean that up, as the cops circled and bathed us in flashlight beams.

NPD Officer Thomas Bell scooped up the boy and carried him back to his parents, cooing, "We got ya, little man, don't cry, we got ya."

Looking back, we probably should have reported the stoner parents to San Berdoo Children and Family Services for child neglect. But that wasn't how things went down in 1968.

Ahem.

My editor at this weekly liked this submission, but not the ending because, he said, "What's your point?"

My point? Not sure I had one. Mostly I wrote this so I don't get a flaming ration around town when I show up wearing my new hearing aids.

My point?

Well...

In the desert, it's important to know your neighbors.

Notes to myself, 07/05/68, 0200 hours:

Can't sleep. Need to get this down.

I need to gather more evidence b4 I decide what to do about Camp X. I used to be good at painting myself into disaster only to pry my way out at the last possible second - I was quick on my feet and lucky as Lucifer. But quick-footed luck is a young man's game.

As William King Harvey liked to say, "The backs and wide receivers can win it for you, but defeat comes at the hands of the offensive line."

What he meant was that if a guard or tackle misses a key block late in the fourth quarter, or if a low-level operative forgets to lock a file cabinet, it doesn't matter what the hotshot stars or the almighty brass do: The game is won or lost in the trenches.

If my speculation about Camp X was accurate they'd need an external cleanup crew to wash dishes and tidy up after the latest Congressional or DoD delegation stumbled back to the blue and silver motor coach.

Some Agency rookies staffed Camp X as a sort-of boot camp, that much I knew. But Camp X was not Fort Benning, GA. The Camp X Commander might convince a bunch of Yale and Georgetown grads - many of whom had parents in the Foreign Service and grew up in homes with domestic servants - to pour drinks and serve food to committee chairmen and flag officers.

However, Camp X rookies would most definitely draw the line at cleaning up.

You might be wondering – whoever you are reading this, if anyone ever does, if I don't come to my senses and burn these infernal notes – why I am so het up to discover what goes on inside that gray steel building?

Despite the mounting evidence against him, I am still a Jim Angleton loyalist. I didn't want to see him done in by rivals. If I'd come to a negative conclusion about the mission of Camp X after only one day of observation, you can bet the FBI had already done so.

I pictured my old drinking pal J. Edgar Hoover – we tossed back two thimblefuls of Jack Daniels one Sunday night in 1948 – ready to pick up the phone and tell President Johnson that James Jesus Angleton had finally gone round the bend.

I had to act on the presumption that someone opened my letter to Lilly; Hoover was relentless when he caught a whiff. But if the G-men were reduced to steaming open my letters home it meant they were still unsure about what they had.

Did my theory about Camp X indicate JJA had flipped his lid? Not necessarily. But it did indicate a certain desperation.

Jim Angleton had warned me to expect an approach from an enemy agent or his surrogate weeks ago. But either KGB Control had a mole at executive level, or they didn't really care what Angleton's CI Staff was up to.

Neither explanation was good news. (Hold on. I have to hit the head and grab a beer.)

Okay.

I have always felt that JJA sees himself as a Christ-like figure, the Agency's omniscient savior. For one thing, he doesn't pronounce his middle name 'Hey-soos' like Mexicans do. Watching him greet a stranger at a cocktail reception was always fun.

"How do you do, I'm James Jesus Angleton."

Say what?

If you can forgive the sacrilegious image, picture Angleton on the cross being crucified, to his way of thinking, by dim-witted Pentagon brass, long-haired journalists, self-serving career politicos and a once-proud electorate now besotted by sex, drugs and the boob tube.

Enter then, in Angleton's concluding moment of anguish, a figure not unlike the Roman centurion who pierced Christ's side with a lance, creating the last of the Five Holy Wounds.

For Angleton that spear tip had to be a memoir titled "My Silent War" by Harold 'Kim' Philby; an account of his misspent years in British intelligence.

The book was published in London earlier this year. I have just finished reading a copy. It kept me up most of the night.

I met Philby at a Georgetown party in 1948. He was a charming fellow; a hero of mine for his fine work in Spain and North Africa during WWII. He was stationed in D.C. as the First Secretary to the British Embassy.

Philby was forced to resign from Britain's SIS - Secret Intelligence Service – after his debauched D.C. roommate Guy Burgess fled to the Soviet Union with fellow double agent Donald Maclean. (I had the distinct displeasure of meeting Guy Burgess at that same Georgetown party.)

Here's what happened: In May of '51 Philby sent Guy Burgess, who was in London with Donald Maclean, a coded telegram alerting him that SIS was about to seize Maclean for giving A-bomb secrets to the Soviets.

Philby instructed Burgess to tell Maclean to flee to Moscow immediately. What Kim Philby didn't expect was that Guy Burgess would flee with him.

Burgess' defection to the Soviet Union was international news, and put his long-time friend Philby under SIS scrutiny for more than a decade. Philby, working as a so-called journalist in Beirut, executed a last-minute escape to Moscow in 1963 when he learned the SIS had finally got the goods on him.

James Angleton is mentioned in the memoir several times. Philby recounts their weekly luncheon at Harvey's where he was astonished at the skeletal Angleton's capacity for food and drink.

Philby said they shared "genuine friendliness," but went on to say, "I had one big advantage. I knew what he was doing for CIA and he knew what I was doing for SIS. But the real nature of my interest was something he did not know."

Kim Philby boasting to JJA of his superior knowledge twenty years later. Ouch.

A later mention had to be even more galling. After the Burgess-Maclean case exploded in '51, Philby was summoned back to London by his superiors at SIS.

According to Philby's book, he met with JJA the day before his flight back to London, "for a pleasant hour in a bar."

Philby continued. "Jim did not seem to appreciate the gravity of my personal position and asked me to take up certain matters of mutual concern when I got to London."

Asking Britain's most notorious traitor to carry your confidential messages to SIS headquarters as he was being mustered home for interrogation? Double ouch.

The most diabolical passage in the book, however, came at the end of the chapter titled "The Volkov Case" which, wrote Philby, "nearly put an end to my promising career."

It must have been a grisly reminder to Angleton of all the lives destroyed by his charming friend.

Konstantin Volkov, an NKVD officer, was the first Soviet intelligence agent to attempt to defect to the West after WWII. He did this at the British Embassy in Istanbul, in August of '45.

Among other things, wrote Philby, Volkov "claimed to know the real names of three Soviet agents working in Britain. Two of them were in the Foreign Office; one was head of a counter-espionage organization in London."

This information was passed on to Philby, who had recently been promoted to head of counter-espionage for SIS, in London.

"The reader will not reproach me for boasting when I claim I was indeed competent to assess the importance of the material," wrote Philby, his pen dripping blood.

Long story short, Kim Philby ratted out Volkov and his wife to his Soviet handlers - and then took his sweet time making his way to Istanbul to interrogate these promising new defectors. By the time Philby arrived, the Volkov's had mysteriously disappeared.

On his return trip home, Philby wrote out a report to his SIS superior speculating about the many ways the Soviets may have had of getting on to the Volkov's: Their rooms may have been bugged - Mrs. Volkov had an overly nervous manner which resulted in endless chatter - Mr. Volkov was known to be voluble when drunk.

"Another theory – that the Russians had been tipped off about Volkov's approach to the British – had no solid evidence to support it. It was not worth including in my report."

Spoken like a true psychopath, Kim.

Maybe that's why the poor souls who are driven to defect to the West have more trouble than the Philby's, Burgess' and Maclean's do when they cross over to Moscow. Soviet Bloc defectors are usually driven by circumstance – they've fallen out of favor, they seek reunification of family, they need better medical care.

Our traitors are simply going home.

In any event, Kim Philby's book must have enraged and mortified Jim Angleton. And made him desperate for a win.

Notes to myself, 07/08/68:

I needed evidence to confirm my assumption that Camp X was a front for a front. To that end I recruited Ofc. Bell for some extracurricular surveillance.

Bell was working the graveyard shift, 11p to 7a. On weekdays that meant he had a quiet stretch after the bars closed at 2. Could we sneak across the Arizona border in his squad car to lay in wait for the janitorial crew that figured to finish up at Camp X in the wee hours?

"Not a problem."

What if some Arizona cops rolled by? Bell said they'd be few and far between at that hour and, anyway, he knew most of them.

"They'll be happy to have the company. There's few men lonelier than a graveyard car copper in the Mojave desert."

What if the cops ask what we're doing?

"We're waitin' on a suspected drug courier bound for Needles."

What if the cops want a description of the vehicle and the suspect?

"None of their damn business, it's our lead."

My grimace said I thought this a poor way of doing business.

"Hey, it's what coppers call a professional courtesy."

You can make a strong case that professional courtesy –
an agreement between fraternal agencies not to intrude on
each other's privacy – led to the wildly successful attack
on Pearl Harbor by the Japanese Navy. Which led to the
formation of the OSS, which led, eventually, to the
formation of the CENTRAL Intelligence Agency.

The pre-war intelligence agencies of the State Department
and the Navy both had solid indications that a Japanese
attack was imminent:

The Japanese Foreign Ministry suddenly ordered
its American embassy and consulates to destroy vast
amounts of codes, ciphers and classified material.

The Imperial Navy changed its ships' call signs
twice in one week, and Japanese subs the U.S. Navy had
tracked for months, suddenly disappeared.

But the State Department and the Navy didn't compare
notes and share intel until it was too late. The attack on
Pearl Harbor killed 2,330 American servicemen and 70
civilians.

So I am not a big fan of professional courtesy. But I'd make
an exception in this case.

Camp X had only one access road in and out so, barring a
cleaning crew with an all-terrain-vehicle, what we needed
to do was park within night-goggle-range of the entrance.

I'd had a difficult time getting Bell on the phone to arrange
our get-together. I must have called him half a dozen
times. When I finally reached him, Bell explained:

"I keep my phone in the fridge on my days off."

Excuse me?

"Cindy's always calling me about something or other - last time she wanted to know where I'd put the stapler. Can't do it, I need my beauty sleep."

I'd seen that w. Helen, sleeping till noon on Saturdays and grouchy when we roused her for a late Sunday Mass. School days were worse. Funny. My partner in crime wasn't much older than my teenage daughter.

Bell parked his unit about 100 yards west of the access road at approx 0300 on Monday, July 8. Monsoon clouds shaded the quarter moon, making the night sky murky. Tho the temp was a mild 80 or so the air felt close and sweaty. Local radio said we might be in for a rare summer t-storm.

In the hour and a half we waited, we saw a couple jagged stabs of lightning too far off to hear. That and the very occasional burst from the police scanner – the female dispatcher had a voice like a tile saw – were all that kept us awake. At one point I told Bell to nod off if he felt the need. He was asleep before I finished the sentence.

I saw a grand total of one vehicles pass by in those 90 minutes, headed east. Nobody paid us the least attention. If Camp X had a perimeter security detail, they were taking the night off.

Then, at approx 0500, a vehicle exited the Camp X access road and turned west. I didn't need my infrared goggles because the vehicle had its brights on. Then they didn't. Then they did. Amateur hour.

I elbowed Bell. "Incoming." He was awake instantly.

"A vehicle just exited the camp. Wait for them to pass b4 you fire up."

"Roger."

"And eyes right as they approach, like we're chewing the fat."

"Yes sir."

As the vehicle passed by I tried to catch a glimpse of the driver and his passenger but the bright headlamps blinded me. Maybe they weren't amateurs. We turned and followed from a distance, headlights off. I recognized the taillights and boxy profile of a VW bus.

My eyesight was 20/20 last time I checked, and I had no problem seeing the VW's tail lights from fifty yards out. What I didn't see was the reason that Bell suddenly juked the steering wheel hard right.

The unit's right front wheel bit the sand, making the squad car want to spin. I braced myself for a rollover, but Bell torqued his way back onto the pavement after a couple of sphincter-clenching moments, and we motored on down the road. I asked why the quick detour.

"Mama coyote and two pups."

I'd been looking out the same windshield, into the same murky night, but I never saw them. Not so much as a flitting shadow. The kid had X-ray vision.

My plan was to follow the bus home, get the address and gather info on the residents that way. I explained this to Bell but he had other ideas.

"Why don't I just pull 'em over on a motor code violation and search the vehicle?"

"What's the violation?"

"Suspected DUI's always good."

"And what's the justification for searching the vehicle?"

"I've seen it around, saw it parked a block from Bob Reese's place. They're all wetbacks over there."

"How is that justification for searching the vehicle?"

"Sus papeles."

"Immigration papers?"

"Yep. We pull 'em over, I ask if he's been drinking, smell his breath and say donde esta sus papeles?"

"Under what pretext does that justify searching the vehicle?"

"Under the pretext that I'm the big honkin' gringo with the badge and the .357."

Wild Bill Donovan would've loved this guy.

I wasn't crazy about rousting some poor Mexicans who were just doing their jobs. But it was whether they were legal or illegal that would tell the tale. Camp Commander Washburn, or whoever was running the show, would prefer illegal aliens he could threaten with deportation if they breathed word one about Camp X.

"Okay, officer, let's do this."

Bell punched the gas and lit the siren and the gumball light. The VW bus pulled over.

I covered the passenger's side of the VW, Army-issue .38 Special in hand, pointed down, puny pen light in my left hand. It felt good to have that familiar adrenaline spike down my spine as I sidled up to the passenger's window, careful to keep a step back.

The Latina behind the window looked terrified, her head swiveling left at Bell, right at me, then calling over her shoulder to the back of the bus.

Only it wasn't a bus. It was a VW van with no backseat windows. That made me nervous.

I jumped back and pointed my .38 at the side door window, which got the Latina to screaming bloody murder and Bell to dragging the driver out of his seat and proning him out on the pavement.

"Come out with your hands up," I said to the Latina.

She ducked down so I couldn't see her.

"Salgan con las manos en alto!"

Nobody budged. I stepped forward, keeping an eye on the passenger seat for unpleasant surprises, yanked open the side door and trained my weapon and pen light at the occupants in the back of the van.

The occupants were three children; two pre-teen girls and a boy who looked about six. They had their hands up as high as they would go.

I put up my gun and apologized to their mother, in Spanish. She was sobbing so hard I doubt she heard a word I said.

As it turned out the driver, Dad, had a counterfeit California driver's license. And a search of the back of the van turned up two things of interest:

- janitorial supplies consistent w. the premise that the family was the cleanup crew for Camp X
- pastry boxes filled with fancy appetizers and half-eaten steaks and shrimp as big as your thumb

Jim Angleton was nothing if not ingenious. Want to run an illegal alien cleanup crew off the books? Pay them in leftovers.

I now had sufficient evidence to conclude that Camp X was a Potemkin Village concocted by JJA.

That was one thing. But the shaggy-haired fishermen sent by 'Wendell' was quite another. That seemed a surprisingly ham-handed attempt by the boss man to convince me his version of events was correct, even tho the promised approach by Soviet agents hadn't happened.

It seemed to me that the Wendell who contacted Jeremiah McLemore, and the Foley artists later on, worked for Angleton.

Which raised an ugly question, the one Maxwell Phillips hinted at in the conclusion of his second article: Did JJA have JM killed to advance the prospects of a dubious project that had failed to stir much interest from the enemy? What could be worse than doing the dance of the seven veils only to have the fat cats in the front row yawn in your face?

Had Jim Angleton cracked under the pressure? Had spending 14 long years at battle stations finally flipped his lid?

I didn't believe that was possible. Not the killing-a-friendly part anyway.

The Jim Angleton I knew would never order the assassination of an American citizen even if he had the authority, which he most definitely did not. Angleton was nobody's idea of a thug. His abiding passion was breeding orchids for Christsakes.

So. What I had on hand was par for the course: a fat stack of dubious assumptions.

(N.B. You may have noticed, dear reader, that I did not stipulate in this report the means utilized to record the many direct quotes from Ofc. Bell. I decided to dispense w. audio since Bell was, shall we say, going above and beyond at my behest. I didn't want any hard evidence that could be used against him if things blew up.

The most I did was scrawl some notes.

I enjoyed the process of creating this report more than the one's I'd compiled previously. It is accurate to the best of my knowledge, even if some of Bell's quotes are not verbatim.

The point being, it seems to me, is, I got the gist. I made the leap from being a recorder of events to an interpreter. From stenographer to storyteller.

Hold your applause for now.)

156

Notes to myself, 07/11/68:

Grigory Potemkin was the governor of Crimea in the late
1700's. The Russian Empress Catherine II came to survey
his territory by boat. To impress her the governor created
a series of imposing village facades along the riverbank,
and the concept of a Potemkin Village was born.

I sent the boss man a top secret cable when it became
apparent to me that Camp X was such a thing. I thought it
a dumb idea and said so, not least because we were
borrowing a ruse deeply embedded in Russian folklore. I
also said it smacked of hubris, which it did.

But, mostly, I was cheesed off that I had been sent on a
mission w.out a proper briefing. After 20 years of faithful
service, I had earned the right to know what in the hell
was going on. I didn't expect much satisfaction on that
score, and my low expectations were met.

Jim Angleton's reply didn't arrive via Telex, tho I waited
two hours at 29 Palms for a response and made another
200-mile round-trip the next day. I didn't get a coded
telegram delivered to my motel room nor a military
courier w. a diplomatic pouch. What I got, three days later,
was a letter at the motel desk from the Needles post office
telling me a registered letter had arrived at my PO Box.

Interesting. Interesting because this was just about the
only way JJA could communicate w. me without leaving
an Agency paper trail.

The return address on the envelope was the D.C. bank that
held our mortgage. The letter inside was a pitch to
refinance our loan at a lower rate.

It took me a long minute to figure out what I was looking at: Jim Angleton had sent me an SW document. Secret writing.

Invisible ink has been around forever but the latest versions are more sophisticated. They come in three types: wet systems, carbons and microdots. The doc I received gave no sign of which type of SW it was.

I worked backwards. Wet systems require complex processing to create, processing that Angleton wouldn't want to deal with on his own. And microdots require a high-powered scope to read.

Which meant it must be a carbon message, where ordinary bond paper is saturated w. carbon compounds that record the secret writing. The cover letter is written on the opposite side of the printed message.

This was all ginger peachy provided Technical Services had packed a vial of the proper chemical developer in my travel kit.

They had not. Now what?

Well, carbon reacts strongly to heat, right? Maybe an application of direct heat would reveal the secret writing. Was there a way I could heat the paper w.out setting it on fire? Well, I had an iron and ironing board in the closet.

The ironing produced nothing at first, so I drizzled some water on the back of the bank flyer and ironed it again. No go.

I scratched my head and opened a beer. I remembered how Billy Chickenplucker had brought up the boot prints at JM's death scene by spraying the hot and rocky ground w. a can of Pledge.

Well, rocks are mostly carbon, right? The secret writing on the back of the bank flyer was buried in a thin layer of carbon compounds, right? No doubt this was squirrelly thinking from a guy who was lucky to pull a C in high school chemistry, but I drove to the grocery store and bought an aerosol can of Pledge.

I returned to my motel room, sprayed the blank side of the bank flyer w. the furniture polish and ran the hot iron over it. Damned if dark squiggles indicating the unmistakable hand of Jim Angleton didn't start to swim to the surface.

It took me an hour of diligent ironing – pausing when the paper got too hot, resuming as the words began to fade – to tease out the remarkable transcript that follows.

P.S.

My forced consignment to this miserable motel room has got me watching a lot more television than I am used to. This is a mixed blessing at best.

However, if Doublemint gum is 'two, two, two mints in one', it seems to me the makers of Pledge should consider selling their product as a combination furniture polish and forensic investigation tool.

Greetings, my friend and colleague:

Please forgive the tortured form of this missive, I thought it the best means for a frank exchange.

I am struck by a particular turn of phrase in your Telex. "Poking the Russian bear for our own amusement."

Whereof comes this poisonous pessimism? Where is the plucky and intrepid Lionheart I know so well? Chin up, old man.

I have always suspected, though it remains unspoken between us, that you regard my conspiratorial bent and interminable mole hunts as a product of my failure to detect the treason of Kim Philby, due to the bond of camaraderie Philby and I forged during our service in World War II and beyond. We had so much in common – from our education in England to our love of French wine – that we were dubbed Kim and Jim, the Bobbsey Twins.

Yes, that was indeed a seminal episode in my edification. But I am not seeking redemption with ill-considered schemes. I am attempting to learn from my mistakes.

I believe that the crux of it is this, and it has taken me more than two decades to reach this conclusion:

It is not the ebb and flow of specific intelligence that will win the battle of East vs. West. What will win the day is a grander strategy. We have the advantage: ours is an open society bristling with creative energy; theirs is a stolid oligarchy whose sovereigns do not begin to comprehend us.

We must press this advantage. We must keep them guessing at all times, even to the point of entertaining outlandish initiatives. This will sow seeds of doubt and recrimination until the Politburo becomes so frustrated with KGB-GRU infighting that they enact an agency-wide purge unseen since Stalin.

I indicated how this might come to pass in my 21 June Telex. Essentially, it is this: The rigid Soviet system cannot tolerate any ambiguity or confusion. They require certainty in all things.

Camp X is a means to confuse and expose Soviet moles and perplex their case officers. We intend to, in the words of a poet whose name escapes me, "let loose the dogs of perfervid imaginings."

That is the singular mission of Camp X not, as you suggest, provocation for our own amusement.

We have, indeed, created a Potemkin village in that inhospitable clime. Our Soviet colleagues will have no choice but to come to call.

Warmest regards,

JJA

This letter from Hal was not written in code, though Lilly's
previous letter had been. No reason was given. – *ed.*

My darling girl,

Thought this stuffed Snoopy might cheer
Helen. She will think it too little-kid for
her, of course, but I'll wager she sleeps with
it every night. Charles Schulz is a favorite
son here because he lived in Needles as a
tyke.

I have heard the desert described as
"God's own cathedral," a place of endless
vistas and solemn quiet, a place fit to admire
the majesty of creation.

Amen to the endless vistas, but the
solemn quiet is a crock of cheese. Between the
rat-a-tat of tractor trailer air brakes on
Route 66, the rumble of five-engine Santa Fe
trains, the roar of F-4 Phantoms from Edwards
Air Base - not to mention the ice machine next
door - a man can hardly hear himself think out
here.

The only silence I do not crave is yours,
my love. Yes, the security regimen has been
increased. I can no longer call you at home
even in an emergency, nor you me, as you have

no doubt been informed. But there is a
venerable option.

I tried the number of the one you know.
It still works. I will call you there at our
established time. Be watchful.

Your devoted swain,

H

Notes to myself, 07/14/68:

I did, finally, receive an approach from the KGB, as Jim
Angleton predicted. This made me feel guilty about all the
dire suspicions I'd been harboring about him.

The approach occurred at the Shaver's Supermarket
butcher counter about 3 p.m. on Friday, the 12th.

As it turns out you can cook a ribeye on a hot plate,
provided you let the plate warm up half an hour or so.
Then you slap the steak down for a good sear on both
sides, drizzle on some olive oil, salt and pepper and reduce
the heat. It's best to tent it with foil to keep it juicy. It
takes time but I had plenty of that.

"I am most fortunate fellow," said a booming voice behind
me. "Sout' Amerika, Nort' Amerika, such wonderful beef."

I turned to see a man who didn't match the voice I
recognized: Petrov Korshavokov was a KGB officer about
my age, assigned to Panama City when Lilly and I were
stationed there in the early 50's.

Petrov had indeed enjoyed his American postings. The
trim, muscular man I'd known had just about doubled in
girth. We came to know each other in an outpost where
nothing much happened. We were enemies w. more in
common than we had w. the locals.

That the KGB sent a man I knew was not surprising.
That's the way it's usually done. I was surprised that he
could sidle up to me in public in an area of the country
that the FBI considered a hot zone because of all the
military bases. (It's commonly known as the USD&B. I'm

not going to say what that stands for because my daughter's going to read this someday. Oh, all right...the first two letters stand for Uncle Sam's.)

But Jim Angleton would have called off the federal dogs, he wanted us to meet. The only thing I was unsure of was what I was supposed to do next.

That my appoacher was KGB wasn't good news, not to Angleton anyway. He said a GRU approach would indicate the Red Army considered Camp X a legitimate threat. A KGB approach would indicate the Sovs saw it as an elaborate deception.

JJA had instructed me to reject any enemy come-ons while keeping the door open. That made sense at the time but, like most things in life, it looked more complicated now that it was close by.

"Petrov, what a pleasant surprise. What in the world brings you to Needles?"

"I am on summer vacation, my friend. Enjoying the river. Bo-tink."

We shared a hearty chuckle at that.

"We must raise a snifter, you and me. I remember your fondness for Remy Martin." He lowered his voice. "I have also a box of Cohiba's."

Wow. Castro's favorite cigar was impossible to get. I'm no longer a smoker, but if Cohiba's were handy I would have to make an exception.

One of the enduring ironies of the Cold War was how enthusiastically KGB officers, the supposed front line of the Worker's Struggle Against Capitalist Oppression, indulged in the fruits of Western decadence.

"Oh, Christ. You're not here to defect, are you?"

"Of course not."

"Whew."

We laughed again.

Allow me to explain. If Petrov defected, he and I would be joined at the hip for years: First as an interrogator during his months-long debrief; and then as his case officer, which in the case of defectors means babysitter.

The last thing a spy agency wants is for a walk-in to re-defect – it's a PR nightmare, and a defector returns to his country of origin knowing way too much. So the Agency is rife w. tales of drunken, petulant Soviet Bloc defectors running their sad-sack case officers ragged.

I didn't have a contingency plan for this confab because I didn't believe it would ever come to pass. I couldn't invite Petrov to my motel, he would suspect audio surveillance. My Chevy wouldn't work either. If I had a cigarette pack mini-recorder, he had something similar.

Crap on toast. All I wanted was a hot steak, a cold beer and an evening of dumbbell television.

"Are you alone, Petrov?"

"Of course."

"Do you have a car?"

"No car. Taxi."

166

"How did you find me?"

"Dumb luck."

"Uh huh."

"Is true. I stopped here to get Coca Cola. It is godawful hot."

"So your taxi is waiting outside?"

"Da."

"But you were coming to see me at some point?"

Petrov shrugged. Of course.

"Where are you staying?"

"Monte Carlo Hotel. Laughlin, Nevada."

"Then that is where we'll talk. Hope you brought your swimming trunks."

I said that because no recording device I'm aware of works underwater. Petrov pretended not to understand but he agreed to meet me at the hotel pool in an hour's time.

I hoofed it back to my motel and grabbed my trunks and my transistor radio - the radio meant to provide interference in case a high-powered directional mike was pointed in our direction. Then I drove the 25 miles north to Laughlin, the AC cranking so hard the gutless Chevy struggled to top 50 mph.

I got to thinking about things on the drive. Things that didn't add up.

There was no compelling reason for me to go to such absurd lengths to avoid any recording of my chat with Petrov. I was only doing what the boss man told me to - preparing to listen to a come-on from an enemy agent. The world of Cold War espionage is a small one, our social circles overlap. We talk to each other all the time. My meeting w. Petrov wouldn't send up any flares.

Then why was my instinct to avoid any possible recording of our conversation so strong? It had to be Angleton's prodding me to 'leave the door open a crack'.

A reasonable request, what you would do if attempting to string someone along. Angleton knew I was fanatical about documenting important conversations; he would want to hear what got said.

And yet, his 'leave the door open' could be an invitation to cut my own throat. An invitation to self-document my willingness to consider Petrov's come-on, whatever it was. That was all Angleton would need to cashier me.

Lest you think the Mojave heat has fried my brain – a distinct possibility I grant you – consider this: James Jesus Angleton is paid a generous salary to be the CIA's Paranoid in Chief. In recent years he had trashed the careers of several veteran officers based on dubious intel from a Soviet KGB defector named Anatoliy Golitsyn.

If power corrupts and absolute power corrupts absolutely, can the same be said of paranoia? Is it possible that JJA, due to my expressed doubts about Camp X, thinks I'm a traitor?

I do not imagine – it's not even possible – that he thinks I'm in the employ of the enemy. But when you have absolute control of a department for over a decade, maybe treason is simply disagreement w. the boss?

Here's what JJA knew for certain: I had expressed grave doubts about his pet project, Camp X. In writing.

I had met with Maxwell Phillips. (I dutifully cabled Angleton a brief outline of the meeting.) And following that meeting, Maxwell Phillips had written an article suggesting direct CIA involvement in the suspicious death of Jeremiah McLemore.

But here's where it gets interesting. I had written off 'Wendell' as a Jim Angleton fiction, a way to convince me the KGB were hellbent to penetrate Camp X.

Yet here he was. The Foley artists described Wendell as mid-40s and heavyset. And both they and Jeremiah McLemore said Wendell had a Russian/Eastern European accent.

This raised a fascinating if farfetched possibility: In his apparent desperation to convince me, and by extension the CI Division, of the viability of Camp X, had Angleton somehow secretly turned Petrov Korshavokov, then sent him off to play the part of the foretold KGB enticer? With Petrov's ample bourgeois appetites, it wasn't difficult to picture him crossing over.

The reason I say 'by extension the CI Division' is that, due to our long history, I am considered by many to be Jim Angleton's fair-haired boy. I don't believe that to be true, but these perceptions mean something in our cloistered world.

According to Maxwell Phillips, JJA was already on thin ice w. the Director. If word spread that Angleton's #1 son was questioning his fitness for service it could damage his mystique of infallibility.

I'm not that high up on the food chain, but it seemed to me that James Jesus Angleton – in his mind - needed to have me onboard the Camp X Express.

The Monte Carlo was a swanky new hotel/casino on the banks of the Colorado. The swimming pool was relatively quiet at 4 p.m. Petrov wore a pair of khaki shorts fit to burst below his enormous gut. We sat next to one another in the shallow end, our arms thrown back along the curved edge of the pool. Where the hell were the cognac and cigars?

But Petrov had seen to that. A cocktail waitress with a beehive hairdo approached us poolside. She held a silver tray with both hands and took small, careful steps. I saw why when she got closer.

The tray held a crystal bottle of Remy Martin Louis XIII. Also, two snifters, a pitcher of ice water, two water glasses, two Cohiba Presidente's and a cigar clipper.

I let out a low whistle. "Louis the Thirteenth, Churchill's favorite."

"Only the finest for my good friend."

The waitress took her time pouring two fingers of cognac into each snifter, then she tick-tocked away on high heels. We would have to wait on the cigars, smoking in a pool is uncouth.

I turned on my transistor radio and spun the dial to a Top
40 station. Petrov glowered. There are few things that
cultured Russians hate more than American pop music.

I tuned the radio to a news station, a better alternative.
Human speech has a narrower bandwidth than music. On
a tape recording, it is next to impossible to separate
broadcast human speech from actual human speech.

The following transcript is not verbatim. But it is close:

"Mr. Schroeder, Hal, I am encouraged that you have taken
such extraordinary precautions to insure our privacy.
What we are about to say to one another cannot now be
used against us."

"Yes. You will note that I have us sitting with our backs to
the hotel in case you have a lip-reader with binoculars
watching from your suite."

"I did notice. But consider, our lip movements and facial
expressions will be reflected on the surface of the water.
Suppose that I have a lip-reader with binoculars who can
do a mirror read?"

"Petrov, what I should say is that I will wiggle my feet to
keep the water choppy. Instead, I will make a terrible
admission: If you have developed the skill and technology
to decipher my words via swimming pool reflections from
a hotel window that is 50 yards distant, Soviet
Communism has won the Cold War and I and the
American people summarily surrender."

We had a good laugh at that, though what I suggested
wasn't all that farfetched. Word is that our Technical

Services Division was developing an audio surveillance system that can translate spoken words from outside a closed room by recording, via infrared beams, the microscopic fluctuations of the room's windows caused by the sound waves within.

"I am listening, Petrov."

"It is the consensus opinion of our analysts that your Mr. Angleton has become a stranger to reason. His Camp X folly is testament to that; that he banished a man of your caliber here to oversee it is further evidence. In a cheap motel, no less."

Yet your DCI, Mr. Helms, continues his confidence in Mr. Angleton – a confidence I feel certain that you no longer share given what you have seen here...let me finish...I know you to be a patriot. I will not insult our friendship by offering you money, though that is what I was sent this very long distance to do.

I will offer you, in the spirit of the warming relations between our two great nations, an opportunity to march us further down the path to world peace embraced by Leonid Brezhnev."

"Gosh, how could I pass that up?"

"I know you to be a serious man, Harold. You must know that if Mr. Angleton has succumbed to his demons, he is a greater threat to you than he is to us."

"Let's back up about ten blocks, Petrov. How did you reach the conclusion that Camp X is a folly?"

"You know the rules, Harold. I have already given you a bouquet of flowers."

Indeed he had. Petrov had revealed that the KGB knew, or strongly suspected, that Camp X was a provocation, a sham. How he knew that was mine to decipher.

Jim Angleton would take this as affirmation of his theory that the Sovs had a mole deep inside CI Staff. A distinct possibility, but one hard to justify given how easily Camp X gave up its secrets to a man willing to scorch his eye sockets with binoculars.

Petrov would expect a reciprocal bouquet of course, but he was going to be disappointed on that score.

"Seems to me that the KGB would be more than happy to have a crazy man as our Counterintelligence Chief of Staff."

"That is a short-sighted view."

"Enlighten me."

Petrov took a long time, and two sips, to compose his answer.

"This is a perilous time for our two nations. Throughout the twenty-year history of our mutual...enmity if we must call it that, the Kremlin has had one key advantage: political stability in your country. We knew what to expect."

"Meaning the Kremlin knew what they could get away with without starting World War III."

Petrov smiled and took another nip of Cognac. "I so enjoy your American plain-spokenness."

"You should try it sometime."

"But I am doing so.'"

"I'm listening, Petrov."

"We look upon your country now, with its political assassinations and race riots and anti-war violence - consider the perverse nature of that phrase for a moment - and we are fearful. We know, far better than you, that chaos invites tyranny. We know that your next President will want to make the KGB the scapegoat, to unify America against a wicked foreign foe."

"The oldest trick in politics."

"Da."

"And what does this have to do with Jim Angleton?"

"Your boss, along with J. Edgar Hoover, is driving this anti-Soviet campaign, with accusations of KGB support for American anti-war groups and Negro revolutionaries."

"Why do you care?"

"Because these accusations are false."

"And you don't want to go back to the bad old days, when U.S. Army combat divisions were on hot standby for Soviet tanks rolling across the Elbe into West Germany."

Petrov looked puzzled. I explained.

"I was a spook in West Berlin in 1946."

"But CIA was not commissioned until 1947."

"1946 was a strange year."

"You must tell me about that someday."

"Sure."

"Salud."

"Salud."

We clanked and drank in the shallow end of the pool. Petrov splashed water on his face and head and cursed the heat in Spanish. You haven't lived a full life, in my opinion, until you've heard a man with a deep voice utter a string of colorful Spanish obscenities in a Russian accent.

"There is somethink more I can tell you." Petrov looked over his shoulder and lowered his voice. "Change comes slowly in the Soviet Union, but come it does. Behold our leaders since the war – Stalin to Khrushchev to Brezhnev. Each one more open to glasnost than the last."

"I don't know that word. Glasnost."

"Openness, transparency. There is new generation in Moscow, men of my age, men who understand the arms race is impoverishing our nation. Leonid Brezhnev is an old man..."

"Old? He's, what, 62?"

"62 is old in Russia. When he dies, we must make certain, all men of my generation, that a forward-looking leader takes his place. That our great nations do not return to your 1946."

"Nice speech, Petrov. Any chance you'll be the new Premier?"

Petrov didn't laugh at my joke. Can't say I blame him. It was a nice speech, but he was asking me to commit treason. I did not, however, slam the door in his face.

"Tit for tat?"

"Tit for tat and don't look back."

This was a drinking game Petrov and I created in Panama out of sheer boredom. We would demand the other recite their government's official cover story for well-known espionage or military snafu's from the recent past.

The point of the game was to challenge each other's powers of retention and, with any luck, pick up an unauthorized tidbit or two when your opponent strayed from the party line.

The rules were that you couldn't ask about anything current and, in direct contradiction of any drinking games I'm aware of, the loser of each challenge had to surrender his snifter to the victor rather than slugging it down himself. This tended to even things out over time.

Petrov and I challenged each other on a host of stories from Warsaw to Beirut to Buenos Aires – you'll forgive me if my memory is a bit foggy on the particulars – but I had the wherewithal to say, at the end of this exercise, "What was the Kremlin's explanation for the FBI's arrest of that notorious Securitate agent in Los Alamos' National Labs in 1959?"

"What agent? What was his name?"

"Press reports never gave his real name, just his code name: Wendell."

Petrov puzzled a minute, then said he didn't recall any such case, which was just as well because there wasn't one. My sole purpose had been to prompt a reaction from

Petrov at the mention of Wendell. He had no reaction to the name.

We enjoyed another silken nip of the world's finest cognac before I asked Petrov a final question.

"This glasnost that you talked about. Is that for real?"

"Yes. Of course."

We left it there. I didn't look to me like Petrov was Wendell.

And now that I think about it, I believe Petrov got his bouquet of flowers after all. That I didn't rise to Jim Angleton's defense when Petrov questioned his sanity told Petrov all he needed to know.

I knew I should report Petrov's approach to Jim Angleton; tell him the KGB thought Camp X was bogus, and that they thought he'd gone bats. It was my duty to do that. Plus tell him that Petrov had tried to recruit me to the cause of glasnost.

It would put me under an even darker cloud of suspicion, but it was what I'd been sent to the Mojave Desert to do. My mission was more important than my precious hide. I had to cable Angleton a full account.

Notes to myself, 03/06/86:

As it turns out Petrov was more correct than he knew about change coming slowly to the Soviet Union. Premier Leonid Brezhnev held on to power for another 14 years. *Glasnost* became the calling card of Soviet Premier Mikhail Gorbachev a few years later in 1986.

(I am typing on a computer keyboard now. I can use *italics*. And, unlike a typewriter, I don't have to manufacture an exclamation point by using an apostrophe and a period!)

Petrov evidently got tired of waiting because he defected to Canada in 1984.

There is one question I have always regretted not asking him: How had he tracked me to Shaver's Supermarket while riding in a taxi on that July day in 1968? My tradecraft wasn't so godawful that I would have missed a Yellow cab on the wide streets of Needles in broad daylight.

Petrov's explanation was that he stopped into Shaver's Supermaket for a coke and ran into me by dumb luck. But he wasn't on his way to knock on the door of my motel because that was far too public.

The big questions – where do we come from? what does it all mean? - they don't much matter at a certain point because you realize you will never know.

The sort of question you want answered when you get old is: How did Petrov Korshavokov pull off that shag job in a *taxi*?

via Telex

TE# 5103491-j

N₀ 53946

15 July, 1968

TO: ROLLTOP

FROM: James J. Angleton, Chief of CI Staff,

           Clandestine Services, DDP

SUBJECT: Petrov Korshavokov

STATUS: **TOP SECRET**

CODING: TSJ-91

I was disturbed by your 14 July Telex. And elated.

I had considered Petrov as a prime candidate for your KGB approacher and had advised the Bureau of Customs to alert me should he enter the country. Dubious of their competence in these matters, I also contacted the FBI field office in Las Vegas with a BOL for Mr. Korshavokov.

That he was able to approach you undetected is troubling. What he said to you, however, is bracing. I am well aware of the disaffection throughout the younger cohort of the KGB with the leadership of Leonid Brezhnev. What I found exhilarating was Petrov's comment that Moscow no longer knew 'what to expect.'

Which is precisely the point. That KGB has concluded that I have taken leave of my senses makes that statement exclamatory.

We at CI Staff are no longer docile protectors. We are now on the front lines.

::TRANSMISSION COMPLETE::

Notes to myself, 07/18/68:

I found JJA's cabled response chilling. Somehow the
physical distance between us made his madness clearer. If
you have ever been a witness to a riot, or some terrible
accident, and read the subsequent press accounts, you will
know what I mean. The initial reports are never accurate.
Such discrepancies are what a reports officer is supposed
to clarify b4 sending the report upstairs.

Forgive me, I'm dog tired and not sure I'm making sense.
What I'm trying to say is that Jim Angleton's cable
indicated that his all-consuming rivalry with CIA
Operations hotshots had got the best of him. Bill Harvey
would say it this way: "Angleton sees himself as the star
quarterback now, not the lowly middle linebacker."

Playing defense is the essence of counterintelligence. But I
couldn't very well lecture JJA on the subject.

I had the top secret cable address of Richard Helms,
Director of Central Intelligence, I could alert him to my
concern. But James J. Angleton and Richard H. Helms
were bosom buddies of longstanding. And Helms couldn't
pick me out of a police lineup.

My only means of contacting the President was the White
House telephone operator. That would be humorous. Or I
could call my FBI contact and reach out to J. Edgar
Hoover. He had the President's ear.

That I considered that possibility for ten seconds indicates
how far gone I was.

Back to the matter at hand – calling Lilly from a pay phone at our prearranged time. I needed a phone booth that had, unlike the common radiator phone, direct dial long distance. I looked around town and found one, in Claypool's of course. I could call anywhere in the U.S. w.out operator assistance; just punch up the number and a recorded lady said, "Please deposit 75 cents for the first three minutes."

She prompted you for more when you talked too long. I know this because I took her out for a spin. I called my bank in D.C. and asked them to check the balance of my checking account. The call cost a buck fifty and the audio quality was first rate.

On Monday the 15th at 10 a.m. – one p.m. on the east coast – I called the phone booth in Falls Church that Lilly and I had used b4.

I hadn't entrusted the mail w. my last letter home. I had used the time-honored trick of putting the letter in a package and shipping it via United Parcel, the return address made to look like a mail order catalogue company. I sent a Snoopy doll for Helen. The package, and the letter setting up our phone date, should have arrived two days ago.

The phone rang and rang and rang. I waited ten sweaty minutes and called back. No answer.

I didn't panic. The package may have been delayed. Lilly may have had car trouble. No need to panic.

I quick-walked back to my motel, thinking things thru. Lilly was savvy about cloak and dagger stuff; she would understand if I called her at home to ask if everything was copacetic and quickly rang off, saying I had to run. I was forbidden to do that but so what?

The five-block walk from Claypool's was so blasted hot that my shoes sloshed w. puddled sweat by the time I reached my second-story room. It was the equivalent of the spy table at a café: in the elbow of the L-shaped two-story motel, far removed from the concrete planks of the stairwells.

I had insisted that our Office of Logistics rent all the rooms on the second floor and the room directly below my own. That's not as extravagant as it seems. Motel rooms in Needles are dirt cheap in what the locals call the indoor season – a.k.a. summer.

I called home. The phone rang and rang and rang. I waited 30 minutes and called again. And again. And again.

Something was wrong.

I had a plan B and that was Leonard Kaminski, the friend and colleague I relied upon to keep an eye on my family when I was away. He lived nearby and was also a reports officer.

His parents were Polish Jews who fled to America b4 the war. They set up shop in Pittsburgh, selling furniture, and did well during the postwar suburban boom, opening a chain of stores.

Lenny was the eldest son - the skids were greased and the Manischewitz was on ice. But Lenny surprised everyone by responding to a campus CIA recruiter shortly before graduating Carnegie-Mellon w. a degree in business administration. He wanted to give something back to the country that had been so good to his family.

Lenny did well for many years. He didn't have my in-the-trenches experience but he was a whiz w. languages - even Mandarin for crying out loud - plus he was a quick study. And there is always something new to learn in what Jim Angleton calls the sublime art of espionage.

Then Lenny's star faded, thru no fault of his own. It wasn't that Jim Angleton was anti-Semitic; in fact he was a stout ally of Israel's fearsome Mossad. Lenny's problem was that he was the son of Polish nationals when a report from Angleton's favorite KGB defector, Anatoly Golitsyn, indicated a highly-placed mole in the CIA of Slavic origin.

Oh, and the mole's last name began with a K. That was all it took to sink Lenny's career.

I'm not saying that Angleton is on par with that Soviet secret police monster Lavrenty Beria. He didn't have Leonard Kaminski shot at dawn. But Angleton did park him at the far end of the bench based on very flimsy evidence. I had seen JJA do that kind of thing b4 and had always assumed he must know something I did not.

But I knew in my bones that Lenny was not a rat.

I wasn't going to call Lenny at CIA HQ and he wouldn't be home before 4 p.m. my time. So I spent a long afternoon in my motel room doing pushups and sit-ups, eating pretzels and drinking Dr. Pepper - and trying not to speculate myself into a coma. I called home every 30 minutes w. no answer.

I could call Lenny's home phone from Claypool's, but he would need to call me back at some point. I couldn't very well loiter about Claypool's phone booth for hours on end.

I had checked my room phone for bugs and Lenny had doubtless done likewise on his end. I had a direct line that bypassed the front desk. But I worried that CIA Ops or the FBI might have some spiffy new audio surveillance technology we CI rubes didn't know about.

For some reason my mind wandered back to Cockroach Alley. That's what we called the flimsy WWII barracks that the CIA was crammed into in the 1950's. The barracks were scattered around and behind the National Mall.

Just inside the front door of those buildings were blind stands that sold sandwiches and soda pop. They got that name because the men behind the counter were blind; they couldn't read any documents you might leave open and they couldn't ID your photo.

I felt sorry for the poor bastards. And annoyed at how they grabbed my hand to take my money.

I suppose the blind men would say that was their way of making sure the right customer got the right change – the stands were jammed at lunch time – but I'm guessing that blind people are like the rest of us: They want to size up the person facing them across the counter. While they might recognize your voice or your aftershave, they wanted the intel only touch provides. Were your hands soft or weathered? Fingernails manicured? Wear a wedding ring?

In point of fact, one of the sandwich sellers had me nailed in two days' time. I was "Mr. Mustard, no Mayo" when he took my dollar.

It seemed like this memory was trying to tell me something. Did I have a 'sense memory' that would help me make sense of all this?

Ah, a pun. Turns out my memory likes wordplay.

I couldn't make sense of this operation by touch, by sight, by taste or by sound. But my nose offered a solid clue. This operation SMELLED. It smelled like the flop sweat at Ted Mack's Amateur Hour.

This simple realization clarified things. CIA Ops was not involved, the FBI was not involved. The KGB was not involved. This was the work of amateurs.

The CIA was forbidden to conduct surveillance stateside. If caught doing so by G-men, Hoover would have a field day at closed-door Congressional hearings.

But neither would Hoover risk an illegal postal intercept of my letter home. Publicity hound J. Edgar wasn't the revered public figure he had been twenty years ago. The Times and the Post were openly questioning his never-ending tenure.

And the KGB wasn't involved either, not directly. If sworn KGB agents were kidnapping CIA family members in Washington D.C., World War III was soon to follow.

Which didn't mean that Lilly and Helen were not in peril. If they'd been kidnapped, as I feared, I was going to be dealing w. freelancers. Most likely resident aliens who had contracted w. Soviet Bloc agencies previously, and heard scuttlebutt about Camp X being a Soviet priority.

Rookies looking for a big payday. Not a comforting thought.

Make the damn call, Schroeder. If Lenny thinks his phone is hinky, he won't answer.

Lenny answered on the third ring.

I said, "The geese fly...at midnight."

"The red river," he answered, "flows uphill."

We laughed. This was the ID code we'd invented, a spoof of cheesy spy dramas. But the mood quickly soured when I told Lenny I hadn't been able to reach Lilly by phone at a pre-arranged time and couldn't reach her at home.

Lenny said he had stopped by the house two days' prior, chatted w. Lilly and Helen and found them fine, tho Lilly did seem wan.

"Wan?"

"Pale, pallid, enervated."

Lenny has a gold-plated vocabulary. I waited some very unpleasant 90 minutes for his return call.

"No answer at the front door, tho the lights were on and the car's in the garage. The next-door neighbors on both sides have not seen Lilly or Helen in the last two days, but said that wasn't unusual."

Yeah, it was. Lilly loved to garden. I checked the national weather map in the Needles Desert Star every morning in a feeble attempt to keep in touch w. my family. Washington D.C. and environs had been partly cloudy and dry the last two days, perfect gardening weather.

"How was the mailbox?"

"Pretty full."

"Any chance they're dead inside the house?" I asked my friend and colleague.

Lenny hesitated. Lenny was a hesitator. "I don't believe so."

"Why is that?"

"I didn't force entry, but I listened at the window of your back bedroom. I used a device."

"And?"

"Nothing."

"Thank God."

What Lenny meant was that his listening device had not detected the buzz of flies on carrion.

I thanked Lenny and hung up the phone. I sat in my motel room and waited for a ransom call.

If only it were a kidnapping, with brown bags stuffed with unmarked bills to be dropped on a lonely road. I would pay anything of course, but this looked more like blackmail.

Blackmail today means extortion based on evidence of the victim's misbehavior. But blackmail has an older meaning. Webster defines it as "A tribute exacted in Scotland by freebooting Chiefs for protection from pillage."

Any payment extorted by intimidation, in other words. Do what I say and nobody gets hurt.

In the blackmailer's mind I had highly-classified Camp X intel worth millions of dollars to the Soviet Union. I would provide him the intel, the Sovs would pay him the ransom.

There was a tiny chance Lilly had taken Helen in hand for a train trip up to Boston where she had an Irish girlfriend, a recent arrival who spoke more Gaelic than English. I barely understood a word they said when they got together, though I could listen to them for hours.

But Lilly wouldn't leave town. Not without letting me know.

I didn't really know what went on at Camp X and the blackmailer wouldn't buy my theory for an instant. I could tell him something more plausible, provided photos and diagrams backed it up.

Yeah, I know. I'm sworn to sacrifice everything for the good of the Agency. Well, I would never put a fellow agent's life in danger, but I didn't need two seconds to decide between my family and Camp X. I would sing like Ella Fitz to save Lilly and Helen.

Simmer down, Schroeder. Think of this as a golden opportunity to sow some disinformation. Why not cable JJA w. this new development and have CI Staff bogus something up?

Because the life of my wife and daughter would depend on the credibility of what Operational Services came up with.

And because none of this was real till I got a ransom note or a ransom call.

My phone rang about half an hour later. I hadn't attached my suction cup mini-mike to the hand piece because a caller w. a voltage meter might detect it. I wanted to go in clean.

I took a breath and answered on the third ring. "Dick Nolan."

"Dick, so nice to hear your voice. It's your Aunt Gigi calling."

In fact, this was Jim Angleton's Miss K. For a swirling, demented instant I pictured Angleton's sainted personal secretary as the kidnapper of my wife and daughter.

"I am sad to report that your uncle is under the weather, the doctors think it might be pneumonia."

"Oh. I'm so sorry to hear that."

"He would very much like to hear from you."

At this point in this clunky, coded conversation I was supposed to say, 'OK, I have his number.' Meaning I would drive the hundred miles to 29 Palms to call JJA on the KY-3. But I didn't stick to the script.

"OK, I will give him a call just as soon as I can. Unfortunately, I'm quite busy at the moment."

I heard Miss K gasp from 3,000 miles away.

"Heartfelt apologies, Aunt Gigi. Bye bye."

I wasn't exactly sure why it felt so good to hang up on Jim Angleton's trusted aide. But it did.

I suppose it was possible this EmCom - emergency communication - had to do w. the disappearance of Lilly and Helen but I couldn't take that chance. My place was here.

My location and phone # wouldn't be difficult to determine; I hadn't exactly been lurking in the shadows. That was partly because I'd been told to expect an enemy approach, but mostly because it felt so good to walk the sunny streets w.out a disguise: high, wide and handsome.

The kidnappers might call my motel room. More likely, to avoid any audio intercept, they would overnight-courier a ransom note, including a Polaroid of a terrified Lilly and Helen.

In either case I had to disobey a direct order from my superior and sit tight.

Had my foolish assumption that I could live like an average Joe for a few weeks set my family up to be snatched? It sure looked that way.

That's one reason why the CIA is so one-way about anonymity: The enemy won't risk their necks to steal and sell back a precious commodity if they don't have a surefire way to reach the buyer.

I kept a nervous vigil by my motel phone. My eyelids got heavy after midnight. Anxious waiting is exhausting work.

Then the phone rang and bounced my chin off my chest. It was 12:18 a.m.

I suffered thru four long, skull-piercing rings, not wanting to give any indication of the desperation I felt.

"Hello."

A familiar baritone replied. "Glad I caught you. I've got someone with me you need to meet."

It was Officer Bell.

"Now?"

"Yeah. Now."

"Why?"

"You'll see. Bring your cigarettes."

"Okay."

"Where do we meet?"

Good question. C'mon, Schroeder, you used to be good at this, making stuff up on the fly. Give the young man an answer no eavesdropper would understand.

"At the place you never go."

"Uh, you sure about that?"

"I am."

I had a wild and sudden hunch about who his someone-I-had-to-meet was. But a lonely spot under a desert moon wasn't the place to find out I was wrong.

We'd be too recognizable at The Rails, Sambo's or Fancher's Shell. The cop-hating Red Dog Saloon, after midnight on a weekday, would have to do.

"Twenty minutes?"

"We'll be there," said Bell.

I hung up the phone and stared at it, cold guilt in my heart. I wasn't likely to get a ransom call at this ungodly hour, but what if I did?

I slugged down a warm glass of Dr. Pepper, put my cigarette pack recorder in my shirt pocket, snugged my .38 special into my ankle holster and tried to convince myself that this was all of a piece as I clambered down the stairs to my rented Chevy.

I parked on a side street a block away from the Red Dog Saloon. I wasn't followed.

A northwest wind had kicked up that made the night downright pleasant. I passed a couple well-lit patrons stumbling along the sidewalk, all smiles and how-ya-doin's. There weren't any chopped-down Harleys parked outside the bar this Tuesday night, just an old pickup and a dark blue Mustang with racing stripes.

Once my eyes adjusted to the smoky dim, I saw a long narrow room. The Red Dog Saloon wasn't much more than a bar to the left, and a few formica tables against the wall to the right, a pool table wedged into a smaller room behind the tables. The kind of pool table where you have to use sawed-off cues.

There were no stools at the bar, just three boozehounds – two skinny young bucks engaged in animated conversation, and an older gent hanging on by his elbows.

The jukebox blared Marvin Gaye's "I Heard It Through the Grapevine".

Ten minutes early. Time to make friends with the barkeep and set myself up in the spy corner; back to the wall, cattycorner to the door. By the pool table in this case.

The barkeep was a stout balding man who walked with a limp. I got his attention by slapping down a twenty and ordering a double rocks of the most expensive hooch on the shelf - a dusty bottle of Chivas Regal.

I told him to start a tab because I was meeting a couple of friends. I leaned in on the word 'friends' because I wanted his full attention if things went south. It was hard to tell if I put that over.

Actually, it wasn't. The barkeep was cross-eyed with booze and exhaustion.

I dragged a chair from one of the side tables to a spot in front of the pool table. I sat myself down. Nobody paid me the least attention.

I use something I call the ten-point scale of plausibility to try to make sense of stuff. Number 1 means, 'not a chance'. Number 10 means, 'damn likely'. Of the three scenarios I'd considered to explain the strange death of Jeremiah McLemore, none rated even a 3.

JM a victim of a KGB hit?

The Sovs had nothing to gain and much to lose. A 1 at best.

JJA had him snuffed?

The Jim Angleton I knew would not be a party to the assassination of an American citizen. A weak 2.

JM collapsed in the desert after consuming too much booze and pot?

Jeremiah was too seasoned a desert rat to succumb to the elements in such a stupid way. 2.5 max.

194

But I gave one scenario a solid 8. JJA wouldn't tolerate an assassination on his watch; but he might well authorize a phony, staged death to promote his Camp X agenda.

Thankfully, my ten-point plausibility scale is so ingrained in my subconscious that it operates independently of my prone-to-distraction forebrain. It wasn't until Ofc. Bell said there was someone I had to meet that the penny dropped.

I activated my cigarette pack mini-recorder even though the jukebox rendered it useless. Ofc. Bell and Mr. X entered a minute later through the front door. Not thirty seconds after that the juke box ran out of quarters.

Mr. X wore a dirty white baseball cap, a striped short-sleeve shirt and shorts. He was a dark-haired man about 40 with a few days' stubble, his face more congenial than handsome.

Bell, dressed in civvies, blinked against the dim as he tried to scan the bar for trouble. The two big talkers recognized him, took a quick nip and ducked out the back door.

The barkeep didn't object. Apparently the Red Dog Saloon was true to its venerable last name. No barstools, no tabs – pay as you go till you can no longer stand.

I waved Bell over to the pool table. He and Mr. X strode forward, looking like Mutt and Jeff. The older man was JM all right, right down to the size 9 boots. I knew this immediately even though his nose was smaller and his eyes looked different from the file photo I'd seen.

JM's plastic surgery was a waste of taxpayer money in my opinion. That's because it had the opposite of the desired effect: it helped me to identify the subject. I knew Mr. X was Jeremiah McLemore because he had yellow-green bruises around his eyes and nose.

We often change the appearance of foreign defectors once we debrief them and send them off to live anonymous lives in the United States. We do it to protect them from revenge killings by intelligence operatives from their mother countries.

What was different in this case was that his mother country was the United States of America.

"Welcome home, Mr. McLemore."

Bell and McLemore did a comic double take. 'How's he know who I am?' 'Hey, I didn't tell him.'

I watched this vaudeville routine with two distinct reactions: a sense of great relief, closely followed by rage. The rage was directed at Jim Angleton for sending his dear friend Hal Schroeder to investigate the death of a man he knew to be alive.

As I said in a previous note, it was now official: Jim Angleton and Hal Schroeder were lying to one another. What I didn't realize at the time was how big a jump JJA had gotten on me in that department.

The relief came because the disappearance of Lilly and Helen was almost certainly related to Jeremiah McLemore's return from the grave.

Doing a quick debrief in the Red Dog seemed plausible given the lack of sober witnesses and the momentary quiet.

"Grab a couple chairs. What are you drinking?"

"Dos Coronas, por favor," said Bell.

The barkeep said they didn't serve Mescan beer. I returned with two bottles of Bud.

"Ratweiser," sneered Bell and pushed it aside. JM drained half his bottle once he got his hand to stop shaking.

"Mr. McLemore, I trust by your presence here tonight that Ofc. Bell has explained that I was not a party to, well, whatever the hell is going on here."

JM gave me a once over with the eyes of a man who had aged ten years in four weeks.

"Well," he said, "that's reassuring."

Bell snorted, I laughed. By rights I should have told Bell to take a hike while I questioned McLemore on a matter that could well torpedo James Angleton's career. But I didn't feel like it.

"Why are you here?"

"I want my truck back."

"Where'd you come from?"

"Panama."

"CIA safe house?"

"Is that what they call it?"

"Is the place you were kept on a military base?"

"No."

"Then that's what they call it. What did you do in this safe house?"

"Mostly I drank beer. And why should I talk to you? You work for the feds, right?"

"Army Intelligence. And, yes I know, that's like saying jumbo shrimp."

"Funny."

"Here's what you need to know: The CIA treats us, AI, like a spastic kid brother. We'd like nothing better than to help you put a thumb in their eye."

"Yeah, okay. Provided..."

"Provided we can do it in a way that we all don't wind up on the CBS Evening News."

"How's that gonna work?"

"Not sure, Mr. McLemore. I need to ask you a few more questions."

"Like what?"

"How did you get here?"

"I paid a smuggler, a coyote."

"How did you have money to pay a coyote?"

"That's a long story."

"How did you locate and contact this coyote if you were being held in a secure location?"

"That's a longer story."

"O-kay. Two more questions: how long did it take you to get here and how long do you estimate your minders have known you're missing?"

"Minders?"

"Your captors."

"I need another beer...I'm stealin' Bell's...that's what you get for bein' a beer snob, hotshot, beer's beer."

McLemore drained half the second beer and belched. "It took us four days to get here - we cut a fat hog up the Pan-Am highway – and the jackboots checked on me every morning, so, minimum, they knew I split three days ago."

"Impressive that you made it back, but I'd like to back up a step. Did a man with a Russian or Eastern European accent, a man by the name of Wendell, approach you, as you told Ofc. Bell before you disappeared?"

"Naw, they told me to say that. Sorry, Bell."

"And why did you do what they said?"

"That's the longest story I got and I see Fat Teddy's flashing last call."

"You know the barkeep?"

"I know most everybody in Needles."

"Did he recognize you when you walked in?"

"Teddy wouldn't recognize himself in a mirror at this hour. But it's a funny thing about booze, you know? Your eyes get blurry but you hear better. Teddy would know my voice if I walked over and said hi."

"Feel free to go ahead and do that."

Jeremiah McLemore gave it a moment's thought, then declined my invitation. I continued.

"Nobody gets what they want if this story blows up now - you don't get your truck back and I don't get a lead sap I can use to smack the CIA around."

Bell spoke up. "What do I don't get?"

"Nothing, officer, the world's your oyster. Now let's go someplace and hash this out."

I drove to my motel after instructing Bell and McLemore to follow five minutes later. The reason we weren't taking a late-night walk in the desert was that the motel phone was my only link to Lilly and Helen.

If I left my door open the boys were cleared to climb the stairs. If it was closed – if I detected a stakeout or Jim Angleton had dispatched burly 29 Palms' MP's to my location since I hadn't appeared at the Marine Base for our KY-3 session – Bell and McLemore were cleared to blow on by and haul ass to wherever it was they wanted to go.

If I was under JJA's microscope I didn't want to know their destination. Our Russian adversaries have a folksy adage I admire. 'You cannot spill from empty glass.'

I circled the block of my motel slowly. I parked in the lot and ducked into the front office to see if anyone had called or inquired.

Nobody behind the desk, which made me nervous. I tripped up the concrete stairs to my room. No sign of forced entry. I put my ear to the door. I keyed open the door and did a quick search. All good.

I left the door open and went to the bathroom sink and splashed tepid water on my face and head – you don't get cold tap water in Needles this time of year. I ran a comb through my thinning hair. Man, I looked beat.

I was relieved at the apparent lack of surveillance but not surprised. If JM was photographed entering my motel room I would be in deep shit with JJA. And he would be in deeper shit with Director of Central Intelligence Richard Helms.

As his longtime colleague, Helms gave Angleton carte blanche to run his CI fiefdom as he saw fit. But Helms was a stand-up guy. He wouldn't tolerate the exploitation of American law enforcement agencies in faking the death of a U.S. citizen.

Angleton knew this. Which is why I believed he had Lilly and Helen placed in protective custody, which he would justify as 'a preventive measure based on credible threats intercepted from known enemy operatives.'

That's what he wanted to tell me in the KY-3 confab his secretary requested. But here's what James Jesus Angleton really meant to say by kidnapping my wife and daughter:

'The escape from custody of Jeremiah McLemore is a mortal threat to my power and my legacy. Due to your local contacts you are the only Agency officer likely to receive news of McLemore's return from the grave. Do not, for an instant, consider contacting your journalist friend Maxwell Phillips with this information'.

Anyway that was the storyline boiling over in my brain as Bell and McLemore climbed the cement slab steps with the rounded stones in them.

Bell made a beeline for the Coronas in the mini-fridge. I tossed JM a bag of pretzel sticks, which he ate by the handful.

The double scotch I drank at the Red Dog must have gone to my head because I had a wild notion. I knew Jim Angleton's super secret home phone number. Why not call the sonofabitch at this ungodly hour, say I have an urgent message, then hand the phone to Jeremiah McLemore?

A pleasant prospect.

But I sat myself down. Superior knowledge is coin of the realm in the spy biz, and I now had superior knowledge on Jim Angleton.

I went to the closet and got out the cassette recorder with the plug-in mike I had used during the beer and pizza sessions with Bell. I set it on the coffee table across from the couch.

I needed pristine audio for this interview. If JM objected, well, that was that. I wouldn't be able to help him.

Recorded transcript dated 07/16/1968, 0250 hours, Needles, CA.

Audio engineer: Harold Schroeder

Those present: Harold Schroeder, Jeremiah McLemore, NPD Ofc. Thomas Bell.

Subject: Lazarus

(The text without quotation marks are my observations - HS)

HS: "Mr. McLemore, with your permission, I would like to record our conversation."

JM: "Like you did with that pack of cigs at the Red Dog?"

TB: "Sorry, Lieutenant, he's my pal. I gave him a heads up."

JM: "And I don't got a problem with it. It's why I risked life and limb to get here."

HS: "I thought you risked life and limb to get your truck back?"

JM: "I love Willie, she's my babe. But I love me a whole lot better."

HS: "Then please help me understand why you returned to Needles."

JM: "To keep myself from becoming a real deal corpse."

HS: "So you thought your minders, once the coroner issued your death certificate..."

JM: "...we're looking to dump my dead ass in a swamp."

HS: "And what led you to that conclusion?"

JM: "This friend of yours always ask such dumb questions?"

TB: "All the time."

JM paused to eat pretzel sticks and swig beer.

JM: "I know too much and I'm legally dead. Why the fuck not off me?"

HS: "So you returned to Needles to get a life insurance policy?"

JM: "Something like that."

HS: "Why not take your story to the local AP bureau in Panama City?"

JM: "I don't trust the pig media."

HS: "And..."

JM: "And I played along. I'm prolly guilty of something or other."

HS: "What did you do exactly?"

JM: "I did some sick shit, man. I staged my own death with a body that wasn't me."

HS: "Where'd you get the body?"

JM: "I didn't. It was laying in the back seat of my Jeep, triple wrapped in thick plastic, when I went out to my garage that morning."

HS: "Thursday, May the 23rd?"

JM: "Yeah."

HS: "And this was all pre-arranged?"

JM: "Duh."

HS: "What does that mean? Duh?"

JM: "That it was all pre-arranged.'"

HS: "So you drove your Jeep to your favorite spot in the desert with a look-alike corpse wrapped in plastic in the back?"

JM: "Yeah. They dressed him in my clothes and boots."

HS: "Your employers had you drive to the death scene that morning, and had you dress the death scene by yourself, so that no trace of anyone else would be left behind?"

JM: "Yeah. And I think they had another reason."

HS: "What was that?"

JM: "I think they wanted to scare the crap out of me. Which they did. Unwrapping that tarp and positioning the corpse just so – they gave me a diagram - and cleaning up after...man.

Worst part was the stench. I know what a rotting corpse smells like, but this was way fucking worse. It smelled like someone had sprayed perfume - like a sweet, strawberry perfume - over the carcass. I puked my guts out.

Thinking about it later though, I got it."

HS: "Got what?"

JM: "They sprayed the corpse with that strawberry stuff to attract the fire ants to do their thing."

HS: "And what happened once you were done?"

JM: "I ran to the waiting chopper at the pre-arranged time. I was flown to an airport, transferred to a big ole Hercules C-130 and flown to Panama City."

HS: "At what airport did the Bell-47 drop you?"

JM: "It was just a strip of concrete in the middle of nowhere - a windsock and a couple of outbuildings."

HS: "No control tower?"

JM: "Nope."

HS: "Any signs of radio, radar?"

JM: "Not that I could see."

HS: "And they flew a ten-million-dollar airplane out of there?"

JM: "Yep."

HS: "Well. They must have been very eager to meet you down there in Panama."

JM: "That's one way of lookin' at it."

HS: "What's another way?"

JM: "They were very eager to get me the fuck out of Dodge."

I decided to take a break at this juncture to let the reader absorb all this information, though the original document did not do so. – *ed.*

HS:　"So, Jeremiah, you risked life and limb to return to Needles in order to obtain a life insurance policy that you can use against your CIA employers without exposing your own involvement to the public?"

JM:　"Yeah. And to get my truck back."

HS:　"How does this life insurance plan work?"

JM:　"That's why I'm here in your motel room, crappin' my pants, Lieutenant. Bell said you'd know."

HS:　"You must have had some idea."

JM:　"I saw this scene in a spy movie. You hold today's newspaper next to your face to show the date and snap a Polaroid – you can't doctor a Polaroid – and that's your proof."

HS:　"The problem being...?"

TB:　"Jer doesn't look like himself. They changed his face."

JM:　"So whatta we do now?"

HS:　"I have one quarter of a half-baked idea but I need to know something first: How did your Camp Harrison employers know you'd agree to take part in subterfuge?"

JM:　"I was broke. The trash-hauling gig for Camp X was all that was keeping me and Willie together – I spend way too much on the bitch. Then they said it has come to our attention that you were a Korean war deserter, dishonorably discharged, and we gotta put your contract under review.

They let me hyperventilate about that for half a week,
then call me back in. My Camp X boss tells me my
contract's been terminated. He lets me sit in that pile for a
buncha time before a guy in a dark suit walks in. I knew he
was a heavy cuz nobody out here wears a dark suit this
time of year. Or ever."

HS: "Who was he?"

JM: "He said he was Miles Saunders of the CIA, said he
needed to talk to me about something important."

HS: "Interesting."

JM: "You know him?"

HS: "I've heard of him."

Miles Saunders is a code name used within CI Staff. If a
contractor like JM repeats that name to another CI officer
– myself in this case – the officer will know that the
contractor is working for us, regardless of what the
contractor has been told.

HS: "What did Mr. Saunders say?"

JM: "That he'd come all the way from Washington to
present me with a unique opportunity. I sat up straight, I
was overdue for some good news. But then he said I would
have to swear a blood oath not to mention it to anyone
even if I turned it down, which pissed me off."

HS: "Why?"

JM: "I'm s'posed to keep secrets for the United Snakes
military and the CIA? After all the shit they put me
through? And then he dropped the bomb. Any beer left?"

TB: "Coming right up, oh mighty one."

JM: "Am I coming off as an asshole here?"

TB: "Yes you are, Jer. But an entertaining asshole beats a boring chump every time."

JM: "Kinda seems like we've switched roles."

TB: "Yeah, kinda."

HS: "What exactly was 'the bomb', Jeremiah?"

JM: "I get to fulfill my dream, my quest, and get paid for it. I get to drive Willie all the way down to Tierra del Fuego and back again. I'm gonna be, like, the CIA's South American freelance agent - have truck, will travel."

HS: "Mr. Saunders actually said those words to you? Have truck, will travel"?

JM: "Never forget it."

HS: "And what were you supposed to do down there in South America?"

JM: "You know. See what's goin' on, report back."

HS: "But you've indicated you disagree with the CIA's agenda."

JM: "Sure. And this was my chance to change it.'"

HS: "It sounds to me like Mr. Saunders knew in advance about your dream."

JM: "I don't see how, never told anyone. Didn't wanna get laughed at."

HS: "No one at all?"

JM: "Nobody. (pause) Shit, that's right, I told Billy Chickenplucker one time. He was writing a story about...something, I forget."

HS: "Did it ever get published?"

JM: "Who cares? Nobody reads that Tribal Times throwaway."

Nobody but CI librarians, who read everything. And who would definitely read any and all publications from the Camp X area.

HS: "And what did you have to do to win this dream job?"

JM: "Saunders said I was to call Bell late on Wednesday and tell him I was worried because a stranger, man name of Wendell with a Russian accent, had offered me money to examine my trash hauls. I was s'posed to say this Wendell guy claimed to be doing consumer research."

TB: "Hey, consumer research, I said that at 29 Palms."

HS: "I remember, officer."

I turned back to McLemore. "But Bell came up with the consumer research guess on his own, during our first interview."

JM: "Guess I forgot to mention it. Shit, man, I was freaked. I was s'posed to leave Willie behind and never see my country again. Oh, and get declared dead and have my family bury a body that's not me."

HS: "Did Mr. Saunders tell you your death would be staged: a ravaged corpse dressed in your clothes?"

JM: "Yep."

HS: "Did he tell you why?"

JM: "Nope."

HS: "Did Saunders say your truck would be returned to you once the police investigation was concluded?"

JM: "That was the deal. But the jackboots couldn't keep their mouths shut. Ten days ago I overheard 'em crowin' that the coroner had declared my death accidental; the stiff I rolled out next to Willie got toe-tagged with my name.

The CIA now has a full-time South American agent – me - who does not exist. There should've been a big jump up after that – going over maps and charts, makin' me a new identity and shit. But nothing happened."

HS: "Jeremiah, I need to ask you a basic question: Are you in or out?"

JM: "Of what?"

HS: "This CIA dream job."

JM: "So long as I got a life insurance policy it beats haulin' garbage."

HS: "And how do you intend to get back to Panama?"

JM: "Forget Panama, I just need to get to Mexico City. CIA has a big station there, right?"

HS: "Right."

JM: "So I tell 'em my story and I'm set to go. The fuckheads in Panama won't like it, but tough shit. I got the goods."

HS: "I think you'd be safer returning to that safe house in Panama, Jeremiah."

JM: "Bullshit."

HS: "Sounds stupid, I know. But here's the thing you need to understand about the CIA - it's like the nine-headed Hydra..."

JM: "The what?"

TB: "The serpent in the Hercules movie."

HS: "Bell's right. You don't know for certain which head of the serpent has put you in this bind, and which head of the serpent can get you out.

If the Mexico City CIA station chief isn't privy to your arrangement with Camp X, and the resulting hijinks of dubious legality, he might ring up his boss in D.C.: And you might find yourself sitting in a windowless room trying to answer sweaty questions from the Director of Central Intelligence."

JM: "What in the motherfucking hell are you saying?"

HS: "I'm telling you to go back to your jackboots in Panama and show them your life insurance policy. That way you'll be sure you both understand each other."

JM: "You sayin' the Director of the CIA doesn't know I'm alive?"

HS: "If you were the CIA genius who cooked up this scheme, would you tell him about it?"

JM: "Shit, guess not. What's it mean that the Director doesn't know I'm still alive?"

HS: "It means that you and Miles Saunders are joined in holy matrimony. If you have a spat and bust up, Miles Saunders - and his boss - will lose their jobs."

JM: "So my hole card is an ace?"

HS: "Sure. And Saunders' hole card is a rolodex crammed with assassins-for-hire who will happily slit your throat and jet pack your preserved-in-aspic eyeballs to Miles Saunders as a Christmas present."

McLemore exhaled and stared at his empty beer bottle.

JM: "You said Army Intelligence would love to stick it to the CIA. What's stopping you? Why help me out?"

For a beer-sodden trash hauler, McLemore was pretty sharp. It took me a moment to muster a response.

HS: "I've been in the spy business a long time, Jeremiah. I've seen many low-level operatives get back-stabbed and tossed aside through no fault of their own. I figure I owe them one."

I expected JM to express gratitude for my heartfelt expression of noblesse oblige. He said something else, however.

JM: "Operative? I'm a CIA operative?"

HS: "Yes you are."

Jeremiah responded in his Irish brogue.

JM: "Well, now, and whatever do you think of that, Officer Thomas Bell of the Needles Police Department?"

TB: "You're a god among men, Jer, no question."

HS: "Gentlemen, I think the cleanest way to get Jeremiah a life insurance policy is a variation of the Polaroid with the newspaper."

JM: "Like how?"

HS: "Bell, off duty though he is, needs to arrest and book Mr. McLemore into the NPD jail tonight."

TB: "How's come?"

HS: "We need something Jeremiah can show his minders when he returns to Panama. Something easily duplicated, something JM's stateside pals like Bell, if they don't get their weekly well-being reports from Mr. McLemore, can put in an envelope addressed to the editors of the Washington Post and the New York Times."

Bell and McLemore stared at me. I continued.

HS: "The corpse the coroner ID'ed as JM was too far gone to produce accurate fingerprints. What we need is a time and date stamped record of those prints, proving he is still alive. The U.S. Army will have the corresponding prints from JM's service in Korea."

JM: "Wait a minute, wait a minute. I'm all alone over here in one corner - and the Army's over there in the other - you think the Army's gonna dig out my print file while their CIA corner man is sayin', 'Take a dive, man, lose the file.'?"

HS: "Good point. But you have a powerful corner man yourself. J. Edgar Hoover."

JM: "Huh?"

HS: "Because desertion is a federal crime, the FBI also has your fingerprints on file. And J. Edgar would be more than happy to provide a copy of that file to the press if it made the CIA look bad."

JM: "J. Edgar Hoover likes me?"

HS: "He might act like it for a day or two."

I turned to Bell.

HS: "Any ideas on how to proceed, officer?"

TB: "I could arrest him for drunk in public."

HS: "And you can do that off duty?"

TB: "If I judge the subject to be a danger to himself or others I can bust his ass in my boxer shorts."

HS: "That paints quite a picture."

TB: "But I can't print him. Procedure is to not fingerprint late night drunks cuz they tend to blow chunks on the equipment. Jer would have to pretend to sleep it off for a few hours before he gets booked and printed."

JM: (yawning) "I won't hafta pretend."

HS: "And what happens after he gets booked and printed?"

TB: "It's an 840 something...."

HS: "I don't care about the code tag, officer. How do we get him sprung?"

TB: "Hold on...it's an 849-PC, detention only arrest. We use it on weekends when the cells get full."

HS: "So JM gets printed and released at the crack of dawn?"

TB: "Yes sir."

HS: "Does he look different enough that the cops won't recognize him?"

TB: "So long as he keeps his mouth shut, no one'll know him."

JM: "And if I have to answer a few questions, I'll give 'em a wee bit of me fine Irish brogue."

HS: "Just keep your voice low and your answers short, Jeremiah, as the officers would expect from a man with a hangover. Any chance they'd recognize that shirt and cap you're wearing?"

JM: "Dunno."

HS: "I'll give you a fresh shirt, and a change of socks and underwear if you like, but I won't offer you a shower. Your unwashed stench is appropriate to the situation."

JM: "What'd he say?"

TB: "He said you stink and to take your clothes off."

HS: "I'll know more tomorrow morning. We'll need to meet about noon, someplace private."

TB: "Got a place. Makeout mountain, nobody there in the daytime."

JM: "Hey, Lieutenant, one last thing: You said Miles Saunders has a bunch of contract killers he can call. Why not sic 'em on me when I cross the border?"

HS: "I'll take care of that."

JM: "How?"

HS: "When the time is right, I'll tell Saunders that NPD officer Thomas Bell told me you came calling. And I'll tell him I swore Bell to secrecy."

JM: "He'll buy that?"

HS: "Doesn't matter, Jeremiah. The point is Saunders will calculate you've returned to buy some life insurance – a credible witness now knows you're alive and will, presumably, report that to the FBI if he fails to hear from you. That'll back Saunders off."

JM: "How's Saunders gonna know I won't run to the newspapers?"

HS: "Because, by the time I talk to him, you will not have done so."

JM: "Man. This shit is complicated."

HS: "Yes it is."

More notes to myself, 07/18/68:

My motel room phone rang at 5:03 a.m. on Tuesday morning.

I knew it was Angleton - he arrived at his office promptly at eight. And I would be at the top on his daily docket, as soon as Miss K served his steaming cup of Italian coffee with two sugars. His calling me on an unsecured line was akin to a cave-dwelling hermit strolling naked down the Great White Way.

"Hello?"

"Do you have company?"

"No. The room is empty; the line is clear. I have been waiting to..."

"Understood. The news is good, we have them, safe and sound."

"Thank God."

"I cannot debrief you just yet."

"Understood."

"But soon, quite soon. How is the weather out there?"

I wasn't the only one rusty at tradecraft. This old wheeze dated back to World War I.

"The weather is about the same. It's been holding steady."

"Glad to hear it. (short pause) There is someone here who would like to speak to you."

(long pause) "Chester?"

My grin reached both ears. Lilly and I had long ago adopted pseudonyms to use on unsecured lines. For some reason, I reminded her of Matt Dillon's gimpy sidekick on Gunsmoke. I returned the favor.

"Miss Kitty? Are you OK?"

Lilly told me that she was fine in a voice that sounded anything but - shaky, hollowed-out.

"How is Scout?" This was Helen's pseudonym.

"She's under a doctor's care."

"Why?"

"She became so...frantic that they thought it best to sedate her," said Lilly in a tone of voice both furious and blank.

Frantic? Helen was almost always upset about something or other – she was her mother's daughter and 16-years old. But I had never seen her frantic.

"Where is she being held?"

"I don't..."

I heard a little yip of surprise as Angleton grabbed the phone back from Lilly.

"Everyone here is well taken care of, get some sleep. I'll expect to hear from you on cue."

Click.

Well. JJA expected me to make the long drive to 29 Palms Marine Base for a scrambled KY-3 conversation at our prearranged time of 3 p.m. Pacific Standard Time. God bless the man, he was a creature of habit. He had given me a precious ten-hour window to make a plan – a plan to put JJA's nuts in a vice.

All I had to do was stay awake, which wouldn't be difficult. I had a more powerful stimulant than the department-issue, cross-hatch amphetamine pills in my dop kit.

Lilly had been about to say she didn't know where Helen was being held. That meant Angleton had decided he couldn't risk placing her in a hospital where admitting personnel might ask impertinent questions.

Which indicated that my beautiful innocent was being held in a safe house in a dinghy neighborhood in D.C. or Baltimore. We called them stooge dumps because they were used to interrogate Soviet Bloc defectors of dubious authenticity with truth serum and hallucinogenic drugs.

I didn't believe that James Jesus Angleton had so succumbed to his demons that he would subject Helen to such barbarity. That was unthinkable.

But JJA would pay a price for my even having to consider the possibility.

Notes to myself, 07/19/68:

Makeout Mountain was east of Needles on Route 66, just across the border in Arizona. It was part of a steep range of dark brown mountains that flanked the Colorado River. Further to the east stood the spiked volcanic peaks that gave Needles its name.

At noon on Tuesday the 16th, Ofc. Bell drove JM and me up the dirt road in his Plymouth Belvedere V-8 with a little more enthusiasm than I would have liked. I tried to focus on a distant spot so as not to vomit, but the road kept turning back on itself.

I got some color back when we lurched to a stop on a small plat of land that looked as if it had been carved out of the mountain by a bulldozer. I pried myself out of the Plymouth's bucket seat and looked around.

Makeout Mountain was better suited to an observation post than a passion pit. You could monitor traffic on the river, Route 66 and the Santa Fe Railroad, from the same vantage point.

Funny how most everything traveled east-west around here: families in station wagons headed west to Disneyland, shiny tanker trucks hauling Bakersfield crude east to Houston refineries.

And when north-south butted up against east-west; when Highway 95 cut across the Santa Fe main line, the motor traffic cooled its heels as the important stuff rolled by – hopper cars piled high with Pennsylvania coal to make the City of Angels burn bright.

Vegas was due north of course, but there wasn't a town worth a mention between us and the Mexican border.

It was hellish hot but I was better prepared this time. Instead of arriving with a canteen full of tap water, I arrived with a canteen painstakingly filled with cubes from the motel ice machine.

I shook my canteen to see how the ice cubes were holding up. It sloshed.

I made no attempt to record this conversation because I was now a co-conspirator. But this is the way I remembered our conversation three days later:

(I'm HS, JM is Jeremiah McLemore, TB is Thomas Bell.)

HS: "I have a question before we get started. Why don't you boys wear hats in this blithering heat?"

JM: "Blithering?"

HS: "Had a long night, I meant blistering."

TB: "No, I like it, that's what it does."

HS: "What?"

TB: "The heat makes you blither if you stay out too long."

HS: "But why no hats?"

TB: "We're wearing 'em."

HS: "No, you're not."

TB:　"Yes, we are. You ever wonder why men in Needles wear t-shirts under their dress shirts in the blithering heat?"

HS:　"I assumed it was to absorb sweat."

TB:　"Sure. And when your t-shirt gets soaked, you strip it off and wrap it around your head like a do-rag."

HS:　"Inventive."

TB:　"Better'n that dark cap you're wearin'. You could fry an egg on that sucker about now."

HS:　"No doubt. How did the booking go?"

TB:　"Perfect. No coppers in sight and Junior Comorra on dispatch."

HS:　"Why is that good?"

TB:　"Junior's a motor mouth. What he doesn't seem to understand is that when you depress the mike button, nobody else can talk.

For instance, as low scrotum on the totem, I got stuck with the FrankenFord – a dinky Fairlane with a 390 transplanted from a big ass Galaxy that got t-boned. The FrankenFord's radiator blows up while I'm in hot pursuit of an armed robber.

Thing of it is, I knew the Fairlane would blow. I kept calling for backup and couldn't get through."

HS:　"What happened?"

TB:　"The armed robber got away."

HS: "I'm still unclear why Junior Comorra working dispatch was good news."

TB: "He barely noticed we were there, too busy running his mouth. I booked and printed Jer as 647-f-PC, drunk in public, then logged him out as an 849 detention-only arrest. And we beat feet."

HS: "Well done. I think."

JM: "Why are we here, Lieutenant?"

HS :   "To make a plan to get you and your Jeep across the Mexican border."

JM: "And say again why you wanna help me?"

HS: "To show up my rivals at the CIA."

JM: "And I should trust you why?"

HS: "If I wanted to bag you as a trophy, Jeremiah, you'd be on a flight back to D.C. by now, handcuffed to a federal marshal."

JM: "But maybe you waited cuz you want to bust Bell too, as an accessory."

HS: "Okay. Officer Bell, what say you?"

Bell didn't immediately leap to my defense. He was a smart kid, he knew I wasn't precisely who I claimed to be. I waited, regretting my smartass reply when Bell asked me if my real name was Lt. Dick Nolan. Bell let me dangle a long time – fifteen seconds.

TB: "Naw, he's cool."

HS: "Thank you, officer. Now, have you boys devised a way to get the Jeep out of the impound lot?"

TB: "I'll swipe the key to the impound lot at the PD, it's an old muni garage is all, and Jer can hot wire Willie in no time."

HS: "But what if the Jeep has been disabled? The plug wires cut?"

Jeremiah McLemore reared back; then shook his head.

JM: "No law enforcement officer in this jurisdiction would ever do such a thing."

Bell nodded in solemn affirmation.

TB: "We got four five-gallon gas tanks."

HS: "We'll need six to be safe. It's two hundred miles to the border and that's on the highway. The safest way would be to off-road it."

JM: "Uh uh. Willie's not a dray horse."

HS: "Meaning what?"

JM: "She's been sitting in the impound lot for weeks. She'll need to stretch her legs, burn the sludge out."

HS: "What if we've been found out, what if you have to detour around a highway road block?"

JM: "Willie can do that, but she'll need a stretch of open road first."

HS: "How much open road?"

JM: "Hundred miles at least."

HS: "But the first hundred miles will be the most treacherous."

TB: "Maybe not."

HS: "I'm listening, officer."

TB: "Night shift clocks out at 2300, graveyard clocks in the same time. But the night shift likes to roll in about 2200 to wrap up paperwork. That hour, ten till eleven, is our window."

HS: "Good to know. But what about the AZ and CA highway cops? They on the same schedule?"

TB: "Not sure about that."

HS: "Because every highway cop in the area has seen a picture of JM's truck by now. How's this? We get Bell to ride scout in his Plymouth on Highway 95 - we'll be equipped with handhelds. If Bell spots an oncoming highway patrol unit he radios JM, who's behind him, to take the nearest exit."

TB: "The night shift cruises at a hundred just to keep their eyes open. What happens if a highway cop comes up from behind? They spy Willie in the slow lane and we're done."

HS: "Can Willie do a hundred, Jeremiah? To keep from being overtaken?"

JM: "Of course. But not in the first hour. She'd overheat."

HS: "Christ. Willie's starting to sound like a temperamental opera star."

TB: "OK, OK, how's this? We get Clovis to run scout in his chopper, radio back to me if he sees oncoming coppers. I ride a few miles behind Jer in my Firechicken to make sure we don't get any surprises."

HS: "Would Clovis agree to that?"

TB: "In a heartbeat. But we'll also need Billy Chickenplucker to ride shotgun with Jer, for when he has to run off-road. Nobody knows the back roads like Billy."

HS: "And Billy's onboard?"

TB: "Shit, all Jer's doing is stealing back his own truck."

HS: "Okay, I'll ride with JM too. If they bag us, I'll take the heat. But they can't bag us."

TB: "Why not?"

HS: "If JM gets nabbed he's in trouble until the local Sheriff or Chief of Police realizes this is a national story about a hard-working garbage man who's been seduced and abandoned by federal bureaucrats.

Jeremiah skates, in other words. But my career is over. If the worst happens, I'm convicted of treason and shot at dawn."

TB: "C'mon. They still do that?"

HS: "No, they don't. It's Old Sparky nowadays."

TB: "Who?"

JM: "The electric chair, like they used on poor Julius and Ethel."

HS: "Right. But if JM makes it back to Panama City, we both win. Jeremiah gets a guaranteed-by-the-threat-of-blackmail annual CIA stipend to roam around Central and South America to his heart's desire."

TB: "And how do you win?"

HS: "I get guaranteed-by-the-threat-of-blackmail job security, if I choose to take it."

TB: "How's that work? If Miles Saunders is CIA, how does he guarantee your job at Army Intelligence?"

HS: "You're not as dumb as you look, officer."

TB: "Yeah, I get that a lot."

Damn Bell and his quick mind. I responded with what we call a lunge and pivot - give your questioner what sounds like a reasonable response, then quickly change the subject.

HS: "We all hold dirty secrets on each other in the intelligence community. It's our currency, superior knowledge. Let's just say I need to prove a point."

TB: "What point and who to?"

HS: "That's my business, officer. But you've got my word, both of you - I will keep my yap shut and give you my complete cooperation. (to JM) You got any money?"

JM: "Twenty-eight bucks."

HS: "I'll get you two hundred. How do you want it?"

JM: "Twenties. There's not much trouble in Central America that twenty bucks can't fix."

HS: "True enough."

JM: "That's how I escaped. I had five hundred in twenties stashed in my freezer that I took along, couldn't spend it cuz they wouldn't let me off the property. But they had a local girl who could come by.

All right, fine. She comes over one night, Nina she calls herself. Beautiful young thing, I almost felt bad about it."

TB: "Yeah, almost."

JM: "Fuck off, Bell.

We do the deed and collapse back on the bed. She's so attentive I know she's desperate. I dig out two twenties and whisper, 'Coyote por el Norte?' She takes the money. And the coyote showed late that night, right on time."

HS: "And how did young Nina slip the money past your minders?"

JM: "Not sure."

I had an idea, but I kept it to myself. CI minders don't consider themselves lowly prison guards. They might do a perfunctory visitor pat down, but nothing so tawdry as a cavity search.

I thought of something else, something darker. The CIA minders in Panama would put two and two together re: Nina's visit and JM's escape. Her forty dollars would cost her. Those CI rookies in the safe house would know their hard-won careers were over when Angleton learned what happened.

The Agency adheres to a code of chivalry – Nina would not be harmed. But male members of her family could expect a very unpleasant visit from the local goon squad.

JM: "Lieutenant, you said last night that I was an operative, so that makes this an operation, right?"

HS: "Right."

JM: "What's it called?"

HS: "Not sure...but here's a thought. It's based on the constellation you can only see below the equator - and it has another meaning appropriate to our cause."

TB: "You gonna tell us, Lieutenant, or do we have to guess?"

HS: "I'm just taking a beat to set up the punch line, officer."

TB: "Okay, okay, we're set up."

HS: "Operation Southern Cross."

JM: "Yeah, I like it. Bell?"

TB: "Not bad."

HS: "Alright then."

We agreed to launch that night and shook hands on it.

Bell, JM and Billy Chickenplucker would meet me at the Needles impound lot at 20:15.

I would be on foot. Bell would drive up in his Plymouth, JM riding shotgun. Clovis Boudreaux would stand by at his helipad, two-way radio in hand.

If there was a hitch on their end, the boys would call my motel room and ask for Tina.

If there was a hitch on my end, I would pay-phone Bell at his apartment.

HS: "By the way, Jeremiah, just so you know: Julius Rosenberg was drop-dead guilty of stealing atomic secrets for the Soviet Union. The case against Ethel Rosenberg was less clear cut."

JM: "Whatever you say, Lieutenant."

More notes to myself, 07/19/68:

The following is a re-creation of my conversation with James Jesus Angleton, conducted on Tuesday afternoon, 7/16/68 via a KY-3 line, at 29 Palms Marine Base.

I didn't risk using the cigarette pack recorder again, and my same-day notes were slapdash given the riptide of events on that Tuesday. However, I do believe this to be an accurate transcript. In the words of venerable German philosopher Arthur Schopenhauer - you can't make this shit up.

I had assured Jeremiah McLemore that I would talk to 'Miles Saunders' in order to short circuit any attempts to assassinate JM now that he had flown the coop. The intent of my message was to back Angleton off by indicating that Jeremiah McLemore had made personal contact with Ofc. Bell - a credible witness to JM's resurrection.

But, per usual, Jim Angleton had another take....

HS: "Sir, Officer Thomas Bell of the Needles PD reports that Jeremiah McLemore came knocking on his door last night."

JJA: "I don't understand what you're saying?"

HS: "Officer Bell says that deceased trash hauler Jeremiah McLemore is still alive, that he spent considerable time with him last evening. I asked to see McLemore for myself but Officer Bell said that he was laying low. Bell said the reason for McLemore's return was that he wanted to retrieve his Jeep."

JJA: "Good God, do you see what this means?"

HS: "No, sir."

JJA: "This is a Soviet plot to discredit us. The KGB has discovered and groomed a Jeremiah McLemore doppelgänger."

HS: "Sir, if he's an imposter he will be found out in short order."

JJA: "Not necessarily. Not if he retrieves that Jeep and escapes south to spread revolution like Che Guevara on his infamous motorcycle."

HS: "Sir, it seems to me that if we just contact..."

JJA: "No, no police. I don't want the police involved. This is ours to do. I have a local man, very capable, code name COOLHAND. He will report to your motel room in one hour."

HS: "Better make that ninety minutes, I need to gas up."

JJA: "You have seventy-five minutes."

HS: "Yes, sir. What's his password?"

JJA: "You have a peephole, use it."

HS: "I will recognize the contact?"

JJA: "Yes."

HS: "And what do you want us to do?"

234

JJA: "I want you to prevent this doppelganger from stealing Jeremiah McLemore's damn Jeep."

HS: "Understood, sir. I will do so on one condition."

JJA: "Condition? You have a condition?"

HS: "Yes, sir. When I return to my motel room in seventy-five minutes time, I will expect a phone call from my wife and daughter. From our home."

(long pause)

JJA: "Done."

Final notes to myself, 07/19/68:

I didn't need to gas up. My return trip from Cottonwood Cove taught me never to take a long drive in the desert without a full tank.

I used the extra fifteen minutes I had wangled from Angleton to stop at a gas station pay phone and call Bell's apartment. I wanted to put him on notice that Operation Southern Cross had a new wrinkle – hired help.

But Officer Bell didn't answer. He and Jeremiah were likely sacked out in preparation for a long night. Sure. And Bell kept his goddamn telephone in his goddamn refrigerator.

I raced my feeble Chevy back to the motel at speeds approaching 75 mph. I wasn't going to miss Lilly's call no matter what.

I had time to ponder on the long drive. If COOLHAND was someone I would recognize through a peephole, he must be a long-serving CI contractor.

Given that, I concluded there were three possible explanations for JJA to order me to keep JM from reclaiming his Jeep:

1. JM's staged death was carried out by rogue CI subordinates unbeknownst to JJA. Angleton did think JM was an imposter and a KGB provocation.

2. JJA knew about JM's staged death and had, in fact, authorized it. What Angleton wanted was for me to assist COOLHAND in eliminating JM once and for

all, thereby leaving my fingerprints all over the crime scene and silencing me in any forthcoming investigations.

3. JJA's paranoia had finally pulled him under.

I thought #1 very unlikely – especially the part about rogue CI subordinates - given Angleton's ironclad control of his fiefdom.

#2 seemed the most plausible, though Angleton had to know that I wouldn't participate in a wet job, much less on American soil. And despite JJA's looney Camp X project and his staging of a death for unclear reasons, I still couldn't convince myself that the boss man had lost his marbles.

I parked the Chevy directly below my room. I heard the telephone ringing from the bottom of the concrete stairs. I took the steps two at a time while digging out my room key. The ringing stopped as I put my key in the door.

Shit. Shit, shit, shit!

I went to the bathroom and splashed water on my face. I grabbed a Dr. Pepper from the fridge and stared at the phone.

If the phone didn't ring again within sixty seconds, I would break protocol and...it rang. Or chirped, because motel room phones don't use bells anymore, just cheesy electronic imitations.

Didn't matter. To me it sounded like the great bell of St. Peter's Basilica.

"Hello?"

"Daddy?"

I had to sit down all of a sudden.

"Daddy, are you okay?"

"Now that I've heard your voice, yes." I cleared my throat. "Tell me the truth, Helen. Did they hurt you in any way?"

"No, no, they didn't hurt me, Daddy, they didn't. What they did was...they made me feel very indignant. Why are you laughing?"

"Because I'm happy. And because my teenage daughter sounds like Queen Victoria."

"Ha ha, you're so funny, but you must come home. I'm serious. You must."

"I will be home very soon, Helen, I swear. But I need to speak to your mother. Is she there?"

"She's right here. But they said we could only talk for..."

And then the line went dead.

Nice. Perfect.

Not two shakes later I heard a rapping on the door that was insistent but not loud. A gloved hand. I looked through the peephole and saw Bob Reese standing there. Bob Reese was COOLHAND. Of course he was.

He grinned wryly when I swung open the door. "It's me again."

It wasn't the sight of Bob Reese that caught me off guard so much – he was on my short list of capable off-the-books contractors – what stunned me was that James Angleton had sent him.

The meticulous JJA of yore would have known that Bell and Bob Reese were fast friends and former colleagues, that they shared a web of what we call an associational convergence, an AC, more rudely known as an asshole convention. You don't want any social overlap between operatives and targets. Putting Bob Reese in an adversarial position in a high-stakes operation with a friend like Bell was an asshole convention that Jim Angleton should have recognized instantly.

I invited Bob Reese inside and asked him for his marching orders.

"To prevent anyone from taking Jeremiah McLemore's Jeep from the impound lot."

"You mean anyone unauthorized."

"I mean anyone."

"And what do you know about who wants to do that?"

"Not a thing."

Apparently, Jim Angleton hadn't closed the circle. Apparently, Bob Reese had not been informed that a supposed JM imposter was intent on taking back the famous Jeep.

That made no sense. Reese was going to face JM a few hours from now. Yes, McLemore had undergone cosmetic surgery, but Reese would sort that out in a hurry when he heard JM speak.

It seemed that I had to conclude that the smartest man I had ever known, James Jesus Angleton, was stark raving mad.

Or was he? (This is what decades of living in a mirrored funhouse does to you – you constantly second guess yourself.) Bob Reese might be an inspired choice, depending on how far down the road-to-treachery he had gone. Ofc. Bell would certainly be reluctant to raise his gun to his good friend.

Cleveland was a horse racing town when I lived there as a young man. Name me another city that has two racetracks - Randall Park and Thistledown – right next door to one another. I spent more than a few days in those beautiful parks, and learned a few things about how to play the odds.

The last thing you want to be is a sap who makes show bets on odds-on favorites - a show bet being a wager that a horse will finish in the money. Such bettors are called bridge-jumpers because that's suicide; you can't make any money betting three bucks to win one.

The only real payoff comes from playing longshots. You want to be a dog player, a bettor who wagers on underdogs. Which brings me back to Bob Reese.

Reese seemed like a longshot who might pay off. He was a gun for hire who had spurned the one solid career available to him. Racetrack touts would call him a Morning Glory – a horse who thunders around the track at early morning workouts, but comes up short at post time.

Bob Reese might be all of that, but I was betting on him just the same. I was betting that Angleton had been employing Reese for a good while, because the one unanswerable question in the mysterious death of Jeremiah McLemore was how CI Staff had obtained a stand-in corpse that had passed muster with the San Bernardino Coroner.

I didn't know how they managed that but it couldn't have happened without the cooperation of someone who knew Jeremiah well. Someone who could say, of a particular stiff, "Yeah, he's a perfect fit."

No, Jim Angleton wasn't nuts. He didn't need to tell Reese about the imposter JM because Reese knew JM was still alive. Angleton's imposter flimflam was meant to set my head to spinning, to exploit my tendency to second guess myself.

Why was I still betting on Bob Reese? Well, for one thing, he hadn't squealed. I hadn't gotten an earful from the boss man about our unauthorized B&E of JM's house.

But mostly it was because - more than Bell or Jeremiah or any of the fine young men I had met out here - I saw a reflection of my younger self in Bob Reese. My much younger self, raw and ragged after WWII. Angry and cocksure on the outside, miserable and lonely on the in.

As an angry young man I had committed serious felonies. But I drew the line at murder. Bob Reese was on a collision course with two old pals, one he regarded as something of a kid brother. He would, I decided, back away when push came to shove. He wouldn't commit murder.

I wanted my rented Biscayne parked conspicuously in the motel lot for the next 24 hours, so I asked Reese to drive us over to the impound garage. He agreed.

I was surprised about that when we clomped down the cement slab stairs. Reese wasn't driving his Bronco 4x4. He was driving the puny, beat-up orange Datsun I had seen parked outside his two-story house in Topock, AZ. Teresa's car, no doubt.

Good tradecraft. No witness would recall Bob Reese driving by in an orange Datsun, if for no other reason than Reese had the driver's seat cranked so far back it looked like a La-Z-Boy.

The city impound garage was a few blocks west of downtown, a neighborhood that was a mix of dust-blown bungalows and city storage sheds. I gave Bob Reese his instructions as we closed in.

"You are not to draw your weapon unless I'm dead. If that contradicts your D.C. instructions, tough shit. I'm the senior officer in the field."

"Yes, sir."

I was also a longshot in this horserace. By rights I should have left a bound-and-gagged Bob Reese behind in my motel room bathtub; I owed that to my partners in crime. But there's no point in overdoing the dog player thing. The likelihood of my successfully subduing and hog tying the 6'4", 200-pound Reese, and of him remaining in that condition until I returned from the Mexican border, were off the board.

That's what they do when the odds against a nag exceed 99 to 1, they make the bet go away. Next stop's the glue factory.

I suppose you are wondering, dear hypothetical reader, why I was putting myself through all this sturm und drang when I had only to wave a magic wand that would make Bob Reese and James J. Angleton go poof.

I could have threatened to take JM's newly-minted fingerprints to the FBI and force JJA to call off the dogs, while blackmailing my way to a fat pension. But what kind of creep blackmails an old friend?

No doubt Bob Reese knew it was Jeremiah who was coming to rescue his mighty steed; and he wouldn't be surprised to find that Bell was assisting his good pal. But it seemed to me I still had the element of surprise. Neither Angleton nor Reese would suspect that I had joined JM's merry band of thieves. Which gave me leeway to step behind Reese when we faced off against the boys.

The drawback to being 6'4" is that it's a long way down. A simple collar pull and sweep kick would topple Reese and bounce his skull off the sidewalk. The question was whether that would that knock him cold or just piss him off.

I was hoping it wouldn't come to that, that we could arrive at an equitable arrangement, as State Department cake-eaters like to say. Jeremiah was the wild card. He had come a long way at great risk to reclaim his Willys. JM wouldn't like it when he saw me and Bob Reese arm in arm.

As I've said, in ju jitsu you're taught to use your opponent's energy against him. Jim Angleton had thrust Bob Reese at me like a weapon. When Bob Reese parked the orange Datsun a block away from the Needles PD impound garage, a way to use that to my advantage occurred to me.

"Operation Southern Cross"

by William Redfeather

February 12, 1975

In Carlos Castaneda's book, *The Teachings of Don Juan*, the Yaqui shaman of the title says that every human being has a sacred *sitio*, a spot where their well-being is assured and their power is magnified. A wise man was don Juan Matus.

Jeremiah McLemore was a 38-year-old private trash hauler in Needles, California in 1968. His best customer was the US Army's top secret Camp X, across the Colorado River in Arizona. In May of that year, a corpse savaged by wildlife was found by Needles cops in a remote area of the Mojave. The body was face down next to Jeremiah's beloved Willys Jeep.

The San Bernardino Coroner identified the remains as McLemore based on dental records. He ruled the cause of death to be "heat stroke precipitated by drug and alcohol intoxication."

Celebrity journalist Maxwell Phillips wrote two columns about the strange death of Jeremiah McLemore that summer. In the first column, he suggested that Soviet agents had murdered McLemore, then staged a scene in the desert that made his death look accidental. In the second column, Phillips questioned his earlier column, implying McLemore's death was the work of the CIA or the Department of Defense.

I never believed for a minute that Jeremiah McLemore was dead. The place where the cops found the carcass was Jeremiah McLemore's *sitio*. No harm could come to him there.

To most of his friends and neighbors Jeremiah was an easy-going guy who liked hot weather and cold beer. And his Jeep. But the Jeremiah I knew was a deep cat. As his only Native American pal, he turned to me for guidance in navigating don Juan's *Yaqui Way of Knowledge.*

I was used to paleface pals asking me to bag some jimson weed or psilocybin 'shrooms to give a trippy vibe to their weekend beer blasts. But JM wasn't like that. He wanted me to teach him how to use the Mescalito because he was eager to meet his "essential being."

I didn't laugh when Jeremiah said that to me because he said it with such humility. I agreed to conduct a Mescalito ceremony at his favorite spot in the desert on one condition: He would fast for twenty-four hours beforehand - no booze, no drugs, no food. Water only.

Jeremiah and I drove to his *sitio* separately, at sundown on a hot and beautiful April Sunday in 1968. If JM freaked out, he was on his own. I wouldn't let him hurt himself, but I wasn't going to haul him back to his pad either. The Mescalito is a powerful teacher, the indispensable aid to knowing. But you have to earn your knowledge.

To quote don Juan, "You will learn despite yourself."

Jeremiah wanted his beloved Willie - his cherry, four-barrel, '63 Willys Jeep – to be in attendance at the Mescalito. Given half a chance, I believe JM would have dropped a few peyote buttons in Willie's gas tank so that we could conduct the first-ever indigenous hallucinogenic ritual involving sentient beings and a motorized vehicle.

I have done more than a few of these ceremonies. Some conclude with an uncontrollable laughing jag, some with a solemn quiet broken by ecstatic groans. And some end in ragged shrieks as the physical world melts down to molten ruin.

The hard wisdom won?

The cosmic absurdity of our puny existence. The profound sensuality of being. The terrifying proximity of oblivion.

But damned if I ever had one where the Mescalito's hard-won wisdom expressed itself in global geography.

Jeremiah's journey of discovery did not begin smoothly. We were huddled around a small campfire an hour after sunset. JM had a hard time chewing and choking down the six peyote buttons I had given him. That was because dried peyote - a small, spineless cactus with psychoactive alkaloids - tastes like freeze-dried shit.

I didn't ingest any buttons because I was on watch, just toked on a repack to keep my hand in. (You tease out the tobacco in a filter cigarette, then repack the tobacco mixed with bits of crumbled hash. It's called the workingman's high because you can smoke it on the job and no one's the wiser.)

When the peyote finally took hold, Jeremiah began to shudder violently, gulping air like a docked fish. I extended my hand. He squeezed till it hurt. I squeezed back.

Jeremiah's panicked breathing slowed some. He tried to sing along with Neil Young on "Mr. Soul" from Willie's eight track tape player. His lips moved but nothing came out.

In a larger, more formal *mitote*, traditional Yaqui chants are sung.

Nothing wrong with that, but I didn't know any.

JM struggled to his feet to go sit in his Jeep, but I restrained him. He commenced to projectile vomiting a short time later. (Which is why we fast.) That was followed by violent dry heaves.

I laid JM on his back and gave him mouth-to-mouth resuscitation, despite the abuse I would suffer if he ever told this story at our local hang. ("First, he wants to hold hands, then, he wants to make out!")

Dry heaves are like a hard blow to the solar plexus – your lungs deflate and you stop breathing. Jeremiah McLemore wouldn't be the first paleface to blue out in a Mescalito.

Oh, c'mon, man. Nobody dies from the dry heaves!

Not usually. Not unless they're amped out of their skull in a peyote panic, at that first gut-clutching realization that your brain is no longer the boss. Your first instinct in that moment is to scream bloody murder, something you can't do with flattened lungs. Which makes you want to scream all the more.

I got Jeremiah settled down to where he finally took a deep breath on his own. And then another, and another. I was earning my keep on this star-dusted Sunday evening.

I said this to Jeremiah:

"You may have a chance to ask the protector a question. If he intends to give you a lesson after you ask your question, he will change his form from that of a fierce warrior to that of a bright stick of amber light. In the words of don Juan, 'He will clothe himself as bliss and not as nightmare.'"

I probably should have said this before JM ingested the six peyote buttons because I don't believe he understood a word I said.

Jeremiah got up on his hind legs a little later and started to walk about. A good sign. The Mescalito is a search, not some psychedelic light show you dig from the comfort of your bean bag chair.

I let JM roam to his heart's content. At one point he stopped and had an animated conversation with a Joshua tree. Another good sign.

Jeremiah zig-zagged back to his *sitio* after a long while. He arrived with his eyes closed and his mouth half-open. He spread his legs to steady himself and seemed to fall asleep on his feet.

I laid him down on the sandy dirt, pillowed his ball cap under his head, and drove home.

I stopped by Jeremiah's pad the next night to see if he wanted to rap. He looked to be back to his old self – drinking beer and watching the nightly news from his green corduroy recliner. He steered the conversation toward the TV. Could I believe the guy who built Lake Havasu City just bought the London Bridge and was moving it to Arizona stone by stone?

I said I didn't know that and bided my time. When JM had had his fill of news, sports and weather he shut off the box. We sat quiet for a time.

"How did it go last night?"

"It went amazing."

"Did you meet the protector?"

"I don't know. I met somebody. He looked like an older me at first and I was stoked, wanted to ask him a bunch of questions; but then I saw he wasn't me. He was my father at my age."

"That's common in a Mescalito. Did you speak with him?"

"Started to, wanted to…but then he changed again, into someone else."

"Did you recognize him?"

"Not at first. He got all dark and murky, like a...I don't know, like a piece of mashed-up crap at the bottom of my dump truck. Then, after awhile, he got clearer, got brighter. I could see the red chevrons on his shirt collar."

"Who was it?"

"Not sure, but I think it might have been a North Korean soldier. I think it might have been a North Korean soldier I shot dead at Wonsan in 1950, so close I saw the life leave his eyes. I felt bad about it because he was a sergeant, not a kid like me."

"Did you ask him a question?

"No, dipshit, I didn't ask the ghost of a husband and father I killed a question. I closed my eyes and turned away, but I could still see him."

"Did he speak with you?"

"Not in words."

"Okay."

"But I think his being there in front of me, even when I turned away, made me ask myself a question."

"What question?"

"You're not gonna see this one coming."

"Try me."

"Why is this Lutheran son of the frozen plains so drawn to the Catholic heat of Latin America?"

"Did you have an answer?"

"Not really. But I had no business killing that sergeant in Wonsan. I was an invader - he was defending his country."

"Weren't you defending South Korea from a North Korean invasion?"

"We were in Wonsan, North Korea. We were there because the North Korean Army had been in Seoul, South Korea, six months earlier. Our counterattack swept past the 38th parallel and kept going. Wonsan is part of North Korea. But that's the thing.

Who says the 38th parallel is the dividing line? Who says there should be a north Korea and a south Korea? Seems pretty clear to me there should be just a, you know, Korea!"

"Like there shouldn't be a North and South America?"

"Yeah. America's one land mass, one continent, like Africa, Australia. The Panama Canal's not a natural barrier. You can drive from Point Barrow, Alaska to Tierra del Fuego!"

"Never thought of it that way. But don't Europe and Asia share the same land mass?"

"Sure, but they're a lot older than we are. Mountains and deserts kept Asians and Europeans apart so long, they didn't interbreed. Over here, we're all mongrels."

"I don't think my Paiute ancestors would agree with you."

"No? You ever seen a picture of a Mongolian peasant?"

"Of course."

"They crossed the Bering Strait to Alaska back when that was a land bridge. They look like anyone you know?"

"Well, high cheekbones, ridged brow – I guess they look a bit like me."

"Yeah. A bit."

"So, you believe that the North Korean sergeant you killed over twenty years ago told you that North and South America should become one continent?"

"Weird, huh?"

"Very. What's the plan?"

"Go see if he's right, I guess."

I wrote about Jeremiah's ambition to drive the length of the Americas in his Willys Jeep in a funky tribal rag in early '68. I didn't mention the peyote because that would have gotten both of us busted. Nothing came of the story that I knew.

It was six years later that I got a registered letter postmarked Republic of Fiji. It was written by former CIA officer Hal Schroeder, who left the agency in 1969. He was known to us Operation Southern Cross bad boys by his cover ID at the time - U.S. Army Lt. Dick Nolan.

He somehow discovered that I was a journalist. He gave me permission to spill the beans about our audacious conspiracy to free Willie from the Needles PD impound lot so that Jeremiah could drive her the two hundred miles to the Mexican border, and southward to Tierra del Fuego.

(Lieutenant Nolan had previously sworn us to secrecy out of concern for Jeremiah's safety. I'll get to the reason Willie was impounded in a minute.)

The triumphant border crossing took place near dawn in the Sonoran Desert east of Yuma. But our elaborate plan to get there – chopper pilot Clovis Boudreaux flying advance recon over Highway 95 and NPD Officer Thomas Bell providing rearguard back-up in his Plymouth Belvedere while I accompanied JM in his Jeep to suggest emergency off-road detours in the event of a high-speed police pursuit - well, all that went to hell in a wink when Clovis pulled up to the NPD impound lot that July night in 1968 in his six-wheel pick-up truck. Clovis was hauling an empty, four-wheel horse trailer.

He was greeted with curses and rueful mutterings. *Why the hell didn't I think of that?* Just to rub our noses in it, Clovis brought along a stack of two-by-fours that he used to make a loading ramp.

Officer Bell used the key he filched from the PD to open the impound garage. Jeremiah hot-wired Willie while I fed her fifteen gallons of 96 octane. JM drove Willie up the ramp into the horse trailer and Clovis closed the door. He drove JM and Willie all the way down Highway 95, then went off-road at the last minute to avoid the San Luis border crossing.

Officer Bell told us later that no one at the NPD noticed that Willie went missing for five days. In his registered letter, Hal Schroeder said Clovis Boudreaux was the true hero of Operation Southern Cross because he took a step back and thought things through.

And he said something else. Hal Schroeder said that his former boss, James Jesus Angleton - who was dismissed as head of CIA Counterintelligence on Christmas Eve, 1974 – grossly violated the CIA Charter when he attempted to deceive local law enforcement authorities by staging the murder of American citizen Jeremiah McLemore in May of 1968.

Schroeder said Angleton paid a former Needles PD cop by the name of Bob Reese to use his contacts at the LA morgue to pick out a nameless Skid Row corpse as a stand-in for McLemore.

The body was so disfigured that the San Bernardino County Coroner's Office had to obtain dental records to make a positive identification.

So said Maxwell Phillips' syndicated newspaper article dated June 21, 1968. Mr. Schroeder gave me no clue how his former boss James Angleton pulled that off.

In the one follow-up letter Hal Schroeder permitted me, that was the first question I asked. In his otherwise forthcoming reply, he claimed not to know.

The second question I asked Hal Schroeder was a broader one: Why would James Angleton pursue such a bizarre and illegal scheme?

Mr. Schroeder explained this to me in eye-glazing detail. It had something to do with CIA Counterintelligence Chief of Staff Angleton attempting to sow distrust among the various competing Soviet intelligence agencies.

I think.

Anyway, back in July of 1968, former NPD cop Bob Reese was waiting for us in the company of Mr. Schroeder at the impound lot.

Reese was a big scary dude with one green eye and one brown. His unexpected appearance freaked out Jeremiah McLemore and confused the crap out of Reese's good pal Officer Bell.

But Bob Reese didn't give us any trouble that night. Once again, you'll have to ask Hal Schroeder how he pulled that off.

If you're wondering how visionary explorer Jeremiah McLemore is doing these days, I don't know. I used to get regular post cards from little South American villages like Asuncion and Villa Angela. They were never signed but I knew who wrote them. Here's one:

"The Old Testament preaches against the worship of false gods and graven images. That always made sense to me, but I may have to do a rethink. I am not the missionary of reunification here in the home of the Guambian people in western Columbia. It's Willie they adore."

I haven't received any post cards from Jeremiah in recent weeks, which makes me nervous.

Keep on truckin', bro!

A reluctant note to the reader, 2/27/1975:

I feel compelled to refute the statement in the LA Free Press article by William Redfeather, aka Billy Chickenplucker, that I 'claimed not to know' how the San Bernardino County Coroner identified the wayward corpse as Jeremiah McLemore.

I didn't claim not to know. I didn't know.

The CIA had the technical expertise to forge a bogus set of dental records from imprints and X-rays taken from a Skid Row corpse. What they didn't have was a way to insert those phony dental records into the proper file drawer of a dentist's office, or the U.S. Army Dept. of Medical Records.

In a case where identification of the corpse depended almost exclusively on dental records, the Coroner would want as many different records as he could get.

As I understand it, X-rays are the key. Dental imprints made with hot wax just give a cosmetic impression. X-rays provide greater detail; the depth of a filled cavity or evidence of a root canal. And, as I understand it, not all dental records come with x-rays attached.

Get to the point, Schroeder.

Jim Angleton needed a co-conspirator with unchallenged authority, wrapped in many layers of bureaucratic deniability, capable of conducting surveillance inside the

San Bernardino Coroner's office in order to determine the parties to be subpoenaed for JM's dental records.

Once those parties were known - probably including McLemore's childhood dentist in Nebraska - Angleton's partner in crime would have to coordinate multiple late night break-ins to replace JM's dental records with perfect counterfeits. And manage to do all that before the subpoenas arrived.

There was only one man in D.C. with the manpower and wherewithal to make all that happen. And it wasn't LBJ.

James Angleton and J. Edgar Hoover had known each other for decades. Both men were much alike: deliberate, detail-oriented, highly suspicious. Hoover liked to brag that he had served under eight Presidents. But Angleton was no slouch at five.

In my mind, Hoover was the swaggering older brother who got all the attaboys, while Angleton was the brilliant, bookish kid brother who felt overlooked. Hoover and Angleton might smile for the photogs while shaking hands at a White House reception, but there was no love lost.

That no army of white shirt, black tie FBI forensic experts arrived in San Bernardino demanding a new autopsy of JM's corpse after Max Phillip's article suggested he was murdered by enemy agents, should have told me J. Edgar was calling the shots. In fact, it did tell me that, but I shrugged it off. It made no sense for JJA and Hoover to conspire in such a dodgy way.

So, as I said, I don't know precisely how or why that Skid Row corpse came to be identified by the San Bernardino Coroner as Jeremiah McLemore. And I never will.

I would like to explain why I waited six years to give Billy Chickenplucker permission to tell the story of Operation Southern Cross, when I had celebrity journalist Maxwell Phillips a phone call away in 1968.

First of all, the timing was poor. 1968 was a terrible year: assassinations, ghetto riots, police riots, anti-war riots - plus a bitterly-fought Presidential campaign and the Tet offensive, the turning point of the war in Viet Nam. Not even Max Phillips could have made a big splash with the story in 1968.

Second of all, I didn't want to hang my young partners in crime out to dry. They had committed felonies.

But the real reason I kept my yap shut for six years was to keep Jeremiah McLemore alive. Once the twisted story of JM's staged death came out, Jim Angleton's career was over, which would cancel Jeremiah's life insurance policy.

It wasn't that Angleton loyalists would suddenly put a price on JM's head. What I feared was that the sudden blaze of international renown would put Jeremiah McLemore squarely on the radar of the right-wing militias and Communist guerillas of South America, and ultimately kill him. As it turns out, I was wrong.

My old friend Lenny Kaminski - who survived the 1975 Agency housecleaning following the Frank Church 'Family Jewels' Senate hearings in fine shape - gave me a down-low heads-up about Jeremiah.

(Lenny enjoyed my story about ironing Jim Angleton's carbon-coded, secret-writing letter, so he sent me one as well; a mundane account of family goings-on. The clue was buried in his sign off: "I Pledge to keep in touch with you and Lilly.")

What I learned from his SW letter was that Jeremiah McLemore was murdered by street thugs in Lima, Peru, during one of his rare stops to get Willie tended to. Seems he refused to surrender his gleaming, just-waxed Jeep when threatened. Of course he did.

I 'd been cynical at first, but I came to admire Jeremiah McLemore's goofy mission to Reunite the Americas. The New World is where the future will be forged. Hardcore Cuban Communism has not taken hold in the Southern Hemisphere. Right-wing dictatorships like Brazil and Argentina are common, but with little popular support they won't survive. Liberal democracy is on the march.

What I am about to say will sound ridiculous, I know. But I never pictured Jeremiah McLemore as Che Guevara on his infamous motorcycle. To me he was more like Paul Revere on his trusty steed.

A note to the reader, 2/28/1975:

I've gotten sloppy at this documenting business. I just remembered that my notes from yesterday - and from 1968 for that matter - neglected to explain how I got Bob Reese to stand down in our confrontation with Jeremiah McLemore and Ofc. Bell at the impound lot.

Like Paladin in "Have Gun, Will Travel," Bob Reese fancied himself a soldier of fortune who sold his services to the highest bidder.

I knew Angleton had paid Reese 50% up front – the Agency does that to buy silence if an operation gets snuffed at the last minute. I also knew Angleton was a canny negotiator. He wouldn't have offered Reese a nickel more than he thought an out-of-work, ex-cop in a small town rated. So I offered to double Angleton's second payment if Reese took a dive.

I gave him a plausible pretext: My report to JJA would state that, when I stepped forward to confront JM and Bell, Mr. Reese was ambushed from behind by an unknown conspirator who clubbed him unconscious.

And what happened to me in this fairytale, Bob Reese wanted to know.

I told him I would think of something.

"You got the money with you?"

"No, you'll have to trust me."

"Why would I do that?"

"Because I'm trusting you. You can ruin my life with one phone call."

Bob Reese thought about that for a moment. "How do I get paid?"

"A money order made out to cash. I'll send it to Bell, that'll keep you honest."

Bob Reese gave me a fearsome brownish green stare for a good five seconds. Then he snorted and we shook hands.

When the boys were springing Willie from the garage, Bob Reese handed me his sap filled with sprung steel and lead filings.

We backed out of sight. Even though it was my idea, I was reluctant. But Reese insisted, knowing he'd be questioned by the FBI.

"I'd rather get brain damage than have to play stupid for those monkeys."

Good one, Bob.

I transcribed the following from a letter penned on the monogrammed stationery of James J. Angleton. *–ed.*

May 28, 1975

Dear Hal,

I trust that this letter finds you and Lilly enjoying life in the tropics. I always read with interest your dispatches for Knight-Ridder when they appear in the newspapers. Your keen eye for detail serves you well. But wherever did you come upon the *nom de plume* of Wendell Cunningham?

In my carbon-coded letter dated July of '68, I suggested that our free and open society, bristling with creative energy, gave us a strategic advantage over and against the stolid, top-down Soviet System.

I regret to say that my aim was wide of the mark. At this, the terminus of my career, I have come to conclude that our so-called Free World is at a distinct disadvantage in this grim and savage game. In truth, I came to that troubling conclusion many years prior, but I kept it to myself so as not to disserve our *espirit de corps*.

No doubt you are wondering about the intent of this letter from a colleague with whom you have had no contact since your resignation. I would very much like to clear the air between us.

Indeed.

In addition, I would like to chronicle the evolution of my thinking on an important subject.

The Agency runs foreign agents in over eighty countries, at a cost of many millions of dollars. Our primary focus is to garner accurate intelligence from behind the Iron Curtain: political goings-on, the states of their economies, their military capabilities.

We spend millions more to crosscheck that information. As you know, truth is an expensive commodity in a closed society.

The Soviets can obtain the rough equivalent of this intelligence for fifty cents per day – which is the cost of the weekday editions of the Washington Post and the New York Times.

And we face another, more sinister disadvantage; one that we know well but the general public does not begin to comprehend. And that is penetration by double agents.

Pray recall my oft-repeated words of counsel on this matter: The key to deception of the enemy is to win their belief from day one. Once you have secured that, you are golden. No matter what ensues the officer who has welcomed a defector will fight like the devil to prove that he has not been deceived.

CIA Operations fiercely resisted our attempts to cement the credibility of our double agents. When attempting to convince the KGB of our agents' bona fides, all we had on offer was an obscure training manual here, specs and diagrams of an obsolete weapons system there. In one instance of singular hilarity, our bait was a copy of the Chairman of the House Armed Services Committee's mass-mailed Christmas letter.

The KGB faced no such obstacles. If they wanted to convince us of a defector's bona fides, said defector would confide the names of his network of double agents working inside our embassies. To ring up that sale the KGB would summon home, and in cases of critical importance, murder their own assets.

That was tough to beat.

And yet, still, it was my belief that we had one crucial point of leverage: paranoia reigns supreme in a closed society. It was my intent to exploit that with Camp X, as you know.

I'm a fine one to talk you might say, but a tyrant with unchecked power, deep within his dark and tortured soul, knows that his position is tenuous; that a younger incarnation of himself is lurking in the wings, dagger drawn. Feed the tyrant a credible story of evil plotting's within the castle walls – indeed, even a half-way credible story - and he will act accordingly.

Recall Stalin's bloody purge of the Red Army and the NKVD in 1938, which cost some twenty thousand lives and set the Soviet Secret Police back a generation. That purge was incited by subversion.

Hitler's *Abwehr* knew that Stalin suspected that Soviet generals were plotting against him. And the Führer's spymasters had a way to ripen Stalin's mistrust. The Germanic penchant for record-keeping was in evidence during Operation Kama; a covert training program for German officers that took place in Kazan in the Soviet Union beginning in 1929. The operation was undertaken to circumvent the Treaty of Versailles' proscriptions against German military training in the use of tanks and heavy artillery.

German soldiers kept dossiers on the Soviet officers they worked with during this training program, noting offhand complaints the officers made about their superiors. Almost a decade later the *Abwehr* doctored those dossiers to suggest a pending *coup d'état* by those same Soviet officers; and cleverly induced a Soviet NKVD officer to purloin the documents. The deed was done.

Those were the days, my friend. I fear my mistake was in over-interpreting the lessons of history; and underestimating Leonid Brezhnev.

Et sic vadit. And so it goes.

I have now joined you in exile; made to walk the plank by DCI William Colby following my ritual humiliation at the Frank Church Senate Committee hearings and the revelation of the so-called family jewels.

Though you and I parted on improvident terms, I recognize that I owe you a sovereign debt. Had you exposed my ill-considered decisions in the case of one Jeremiah McLemore at the time of their occurrence, I would not have been in place to coordinate investigations of Soviet agents seeking to penetrate and capture our negotiating agenda in the Strategic Arms Limitations Talks and the subsequent Anti-Ballistic Missile Treaty.

And that is not to mention the fierce and unending Soviet attempts to sabotage President Nixon's visit to Red China.

I was able to oversee all three of those victorious accomplishments, though I grant you oversee may sound a bit vainglorious.

Let me say, simply, that I was able to make important contributions to the Agency's mission in the six years that you granted me.

Thank you, good sir.

We have done our utmost, you and I. We did not succumb to that perfidy, about which the Poet warned:

"Our doubts are traitors, and make us lose the good we oft might win by fearing to attempt."

Yours sincerely,

Jim

I transcribed the following from a handwritten draft of Hal Schroeder's reply to James Angleton's letter dated May 28, 1975. – *ed.*

Dear Jim,

I was more than a little surprised to receive your congenial correspondence. I especially appreciated your candor and humility with regard to the staged death of Jeremiah McLemore.

I would like to clear the air between us as well. To wit: What in the name of God were you thinking when you cooked up that preposterous scheme?

More to the point, why did you send your good and trusted friend Hal Schroeder on that fool's errand? That you saw fit to take my wife and daughter into protective custody during that time was, and remains, unforgiveable.

No doubt you think I acted foolishly in abetting Jeremiah McLemore's escape. In retrospect, risking my career to reunite a stranger with his prized possession does seem a dumb stunt. And yet I would do it again.

I will return to that thought in a moment, but let's consider a bigger question: I believe the Frank Church Committee hearings, for all their pomposity, were a much-needed bloodletting. Keeping dossiers on American citizens for the crime of opposing the Viet Nam War was a serious violation of our charter; something one would expect of the

Warsaw Pact. Ditto attempting to overthrow democratically elected governments.

Yes, I did once embrace OSS Chief Wild Bill Donovan's 'try anything' attitude. But that was during WWII, and those crazy post-war years when the American public didn't begin to get the enormity of the Soviet threat.

They do now. And if the global tale we're trying to tell is that the Yanks are the white hats and the Commies the black hats, well, we should have backed that up with good behavior. Instead we got fat and happy and became a parody of ourselves - not 007 but Maxwell Smart.

You need not thank me for keeping my mouth shut about Jeremiah McLemore when I resigned in '69. I did it for selfish reasons. I wanted to spare my family the pain of congressional hearings and the resulting circus. I wanted to situate my daughter in the college of her choice and get the hell out.

Lilly and I moved to Fiji, a pipedream of mine since my frozen childhood in Youngstown. Helen graduated Skidmore last year, with honors. We're in good shape.

Back to your letter...

I am sincerely pleased that you were able to play an important part in the remarkable progress we have made in reducing tensions with the Soviets and Red China. In the span of just a dozen years the specter of a nuclear cataclysm - so gut-clenching during the Cuban Missile Crisis - is now almost unthinkable.

We all deserve some credit for that. Even the State Department cake-eaters should step forward and take a bow.

Years ago I told you I thought Camp X a Potemkin Village; but now I think that metaphor more properly belongs in Russia where it began. There were many Potemkin villages, not just one. Grigory Potemkin struck the façade of the prosperous village after the royal barge passed by. While the barge docked for the night, Potemkin's men drove wagons containing the false fronts to the next destination downstream; then reassembled them at dawn before Empress Catherine floated past.

I think Soviet Communism has been doing that for a long time, creating the illusion of prosperity for the wider world to see. We know the Soviet system is corrupt, brutal and unworkable; but I believe the Russian people are finally beginning to see that too.

Of course the Russians are famously stoic; willing to stand on queue for hours in a deep freeze to collect sausage made of straw and pig guts as the Wehrmacht bore down on Moscow. Now that the Great Patriotic War is over and the Victory of the Proletariat assured, however, not much has changed. The quality of the sausage may have improved; but the wait is still long and the national mood bleak.

In short, I believe the Soviet system will collapse under the weight of its own contradictions within our lifetimes. And that will be a fine day.

Jim, I too will close with a quote from Shakespeare. It's from Macbeth, and should be, in this man's opinion, chiseled in granite on the wall of the front lobby at Langley:

"Cruel are the times when we are traitors and do not know ourselves, when we hold rumor from what we fear, yet know not what we fear, but float upon a wild and violent sea."

Neither a date nor a signature was appended to this handwritten letter. It is not known if a typewritten version was ever sent. – *ed.*

EPILOGUE

I am Helen, Harold and Lilly Schroeder's only child, and I am writing this in the winter of 2005. I am the one who compiled this book, the *ed.* who popped up occasionally.

My father died earlier this year, on January 10th, a year after he lost his beloved Lilly to a sudden and fatal brain tumor. He was 83. I last saw him at Christmastime. My parents moved to Fiji in 1969 but they always made the long flights home for the holidays.

I am married to Tim O'Donnell, a hotel manager and wicked fiddle player, and we have two grown kids, Colin and Jessica. I inherited my father's love of food and run a thriving gourmet market and cafe in Annapolis, Maryland, our home.

My father's final visit was very pleasant. He reminisced about Mom quite a bit, but in a happy way. He said he was feeling fit and looked the part with his South Seas tan. But he was gaunt. I tried to fatten him up the best I could.

I didn't ask him to stay with us now that Mom was gone, I knew what the answer would be. And when we said goodbye at the airport I knew I wouldn't see him again. His hug went on far too long.

My father's doctor in Fiji reported that he died of heart failure and I suppose that's true. But what really killed him was grief.

This spring I found a small, portable safe in my potting shed, hidden under a bag of mulch. I knew immediately that Dad had put it there but how he managed to do that without my knowing I cannot begin to tell you.

I tried the obvious three double digit combinations – family birthdays and dates of death – without success. But of course it would be a date that only I would know. When I was a girl we would always have a quiet celebration, just the three of us, of that day in 1948 when Hal met Lilly at the Mooney Brothers Bar & Grill in the city of Cork.

When I tried that date the safe popped open. Inside I found a stack of vacuum-wrapped pages, a separate spiral-bound notebook, letters sealed in a Ziploc bag and, on top of the pile, a yellowed typewritten page carefully tucked into a plastic sleeve.

The page on top was quite old, the edges nibbled by termites. No instructions there. I opened the vacuum-sealed stack of pages underneath to find typewritten notes, official documents and newspaper articles, mostly dated from 1968. Beneath that was a spiral-bound notebook that contained one and two-page entries in my father's cramped hand, also mostly dated 1968.

I searched through all the papers but found no instructions. Apparently, my father expected me to piece this jigsaw together all by myself.

I was cursing his stubbornness – he who always claimed that women were the stubborn sex - when I noticed a folded crag of paper that was stuck to the bottom of the vacuum-wrapped pages. It was a recent handwritten letter addressed to me.

Dollface,

You are the only one still living I can entrust this to. I have outlived the few colleagues I trusted. Even fun-loving rookie cop Thomas Bell is gone, killed in action in California years ago.

This is not a deathbed request, you do not have to tell this story to the wider world. But you were always so curious about my work when you were a loveable doe-eyed tyrant that I am pleased that now, finally, I can share some of it with you. Pleased and deeply embarrassed as you will see.

This material has some historical significance but is too old to have any strategic value. However, as my Russian friend Petrov liked to say, Cuban cigar in one hand, glass of cognac in the other, "One never knows, does one?"

In other words, if you decide not to tackle this pile of insanity please make sure that it is properly destroyed - burned, the ashes scattered. I wouldn't want this material to fall into the hands of those who might cannibalize it to promote a political agenda.

Make an afternoon of it, you and Tim. Say your goodbyes. You were short-changed in that department since you didn't get to attend our funerals. As you know Lilly insisted on a brief, low key ceremony because she didn't want you and your family to suffer an exhausting trip on her account.

Me too. We had our time together at Christmas.

Here's the storyline: When I entered the Agency in 1948 we had no effective counterintelligence to speak of. When I left twenty years later our CI Staff had turned the Agency into a snake pit of paranoia. That is what these documents have captured in a small way.

Sorry to dump this on your bony head, dear girl. I suppose I should have published it myself but that felt too self-serving. I was not interested in reclaiming my good name after all these years. When I abruptly resigned in early '69, and Lilly and I moved halfway around the world, most of the Agency assumed Jim Angleton had canned me for some screw-up because Camp X was shuttered about that time.

But my name wasn't tarnished so far as anyone I knew and respected was concerned.

I have always considered myself a lucky man in an unlucky world. I was the only OSS agent to survive service behind German lines in WWII. I never spoke of that out of respect for those who did not return.

You should also know that I recruited your dear uncles, Ambrose, Sean and Patrick, to help me rob the Federal Reserve Bank of Cleveland in 1945. An unforgiveable act that I regret to this day. No one innocent died as a result, but a good man's reputation was ruined. And I walked away a hero. Ridiculous.

I was an angry young man after all I had seen in that terrible war. Nowadays they would say I was suffering from Post-Traumatic Stress Syndrome and give me a pass. But I saw a few cases of what we used to call shell shock and that wasn't me. I knew what I was doing.

I never spoke of this to you because you always seemed so proud of me and I was always a coward where you were concerned. Perhaps your mother told you. I don't know because I was afraid to ask.

So that is what you need to know about your dear departed daddy.

My luck held when you were born. Best day of my life and Lilly's too. We had suffered through two miscarriages and thought we had lost you too when Lilly started spotting at three months. (I learned more about female biology in those years than I ever cared to know.) But you came yammering to life six months later, right on schedule.

I was a fallen Catholic at that point in my life, but I went down to the Cathedral of St. Matthew's and prayed three rosaries on my knees that day. And I have been a, mostly, observant penitent ever since.

No, this is not a deathbed request, it's worse - it's beyond-the-grave. Do what you will with what I have left you and, if you decide to proceed, feel free to correct my grammar.

Love always and forever (and, yes, I know that's redundant),

Dad

I didn't know what to make of all this...stuff. Mom never told me about the bank robbery and my uncles never said a word, though we visited them in Cork every few years.

I knew that Sean and Patrick helped Dad rescue Ambrose from the Soviets in Berlin in 1946, they weren't shy about that. But they were vague about why they never came to see us in the States.

I was angry with my father for dumping this on me when I could no longer ask him why in the world he had done such a terrible thing.

No one innocent was killed? Why was *anyone* killed?

I shoved the documents back in the safe, thinking my father's suggestion of scattering their burning ashes a good one.

But I relented. He was a good father and a decent man. And I never could resist a jigsaw puzzle.

Feel free to draw your own conclusions, but I do believe Dad was spot on about James Jesus Angleton. I read up on him. The man was a well-intentioned genius who lost himself in his own imaginings, in what author David Martin called his "Wilderness of Mirrors", a phrase he borrowed from T.S. Eliot, one of the young Angleton's literary heroes.

James Angleton cost many upstanding agents their careers, men who carried the stigma of suspicion the rest of their lives. As Hal Schroeder did after his resignation.

Dad was eventually proved right. Angleton was fired in 1974 and the Senate Committee hearings chaired by Frank Church partially exposed the madhouse that the CIA had become.

My father could have returned triumphant from his exile. He could have testified in front of the Church Committee and told the strange saga of Jeremiah McLemore to illustrate just how divorced from reality James Angleton had become.

But my father didn't do that. He was, for better or for worse, a good soldier.

The one insoluble mystery in my father's fat stack of documents is the one on top. The termite-chewed typewritten page in the plastic sleeve. The one that says, "You die of heat, it's torture."

The typewriter used was an old Smith Corona, back when 'pounding out pages' meant just that. I know because I hired one Raymond Briare, a retired forensic document investigator, who concluded that the page had been pounded out on cheap stationary circa 1948 or '49.

Briare used software to crosscheck the wording and sentence structure on the tattered page to an enormous database of published American authors and poets. He concluded that the writer was an unknown contributor.

I think that someone gave this venerable page to my father, some sun-blind poet/prospector who stopped by The Rails and he and Dad got to talking. My father paid the tab and the poet/prospector thanked him with the typewritten, single-page currency he kept in his rucksack.

That's the way I like to picture it anyway. Dad didn't share it with Mom because she hated those six weeks in 1968 when he disappeared. I believe my father saved the termite-chewed meditation on the Mojave Desert as a gift for me: a consolation prize for the Bobby Kennedy memento I never received.

There is one more mystery that my father's notes do not address. In his notes dated June 18th, 1968, he said he had learned not to get too cute with elaborate undercover stories so as not to forget a crucial detail and "expose your country to nuclear annihilation."

Dad? How could you not explain that?!

I assumed it was a reference to the Cuban Missile Crisis. My research indicated that James Angleton was not involved in that terrifying standoff with the Soviets though Bill Harvey, Dad's previous boss, was. Harvey was running Cuban expatriates out of Miami in 1963, sending them across the Straits of Florida on nighttime sabotage missions.

But my father was a reports officer working for Angleton in 1963, not a case officer working for Harvey. Was he working for Bill Harvey off-the-books? Or was there a much earlier moment of terrifying nuclear confrontation between the superpowers that the public doesn't know about?

Godspeed, Daddy.

I appreciate you sharing what you could, but you won out in the end: You died with superior knowledge.

--*Helen O'Donnell*

The following is an article my father wrote in tribute to Officer Thomas Bell after he learned of his death in the line of duty in 1994. Bell was the rookie cop my father so enjoyed working with in Needles.

I learned that Bell had a successful radio career but eventually returned to police work in the small coastal town of Winslow, California in 1989. In a bitter irony my father must have felt, Bell, who was a training officer at the time, was accidentally shot and killed by a rookie cop.

I found the grainy photo below in a manila envelope along with the article. It isn't marked in any way, but it has to be Officer Bell.

282

That my father knew all the details of this hair-raising call in Needles indicates to me that he was riding with Bell that night.

Winslow Register

The following is a true story told in tribute to my recently deceased friend and former colleague, Officer Thomas A. Bell...

The Mojave Desert can get cold at night even in the summertime. Dry air and soil don't hold the daytime heat through the night when the mountain winds are blowing. So that hour before dawn in June of 1968 was downright chilly when 21-year-old Needles P.D. officer Thomas Bell, working the graveyard shift, responded to a neighbor's call of a domestic dispute in a residential neighborhood.

Bell rolled up to find a modest desert hacienda with a California Highway Patrol unit parked in front. Bell unholstered his .357 as he ran toward the sound of angry voices from the fenced-in backyard. At 6'4" he didn't need to stand on tiptoe to survey the scene.

What he glimmed in the pale dark was a white male – 5'9", 150 lbs., late 20's – swearing a blue streak and brandishing a double barrel twelve-gauge shotgun, double cocked for immediate action. On the far side of the yard, behind the wooden fence, Bell saw a young CHP officer brandishing only a small-caliber sixgun.

The white male was directing his curses at a blowsy woman in her 30's who returned the favor from a back window. She appeared unarmed. From their back and forth Bell gathered that they were a one-night-stand gone wrong.

Both Bell and the CHP officer continued to repeat, "Drop the weapon, drop the weapon," without success.

At one point the white male suspect turned and pointed his shotgun at Bell's face.

Bell, a rookie at the time, hesitated; though he was well within his rights to pump all six rounds into the subject.

It was a good thing he held up because NPD sergeant Bruce Weekly chose that moment to step into Bell's line of fire.

Weekly, who had arrived to provide backup, had slipped inside the back of the backyard fence and crept up on the shotgun-wielding man, unaware that Bell - behind the fence and to Weekly's left - was a breath away from opening fire.

The male subject ran out of steam once he saw the cops had him triangulated. He dropped his twin-barrel and got cuffed without a struggle, saying, "Aww crap. I should never drink."

The cops placed the subject in the back of Bell's squad car, and all three cops drove separately to the Needles Police Department as pink dawn crept over the horizon.

When Bell opened the back seat outside the NPD booking station the white male subject whom Bell described as "a scrappy, hard-muscled railroad bo," was curled into a tight ball against the far door.

"I saw the face of Satan for the first time that morning," Bell said later. "All three of us stood at the open car door while the guy hissed...

"You'll never get me out of the car."

And it took the three cops, all of whom were far larger than the handcuffed subject, a good fifteen minutes to extricate him, writhing and bucking, from the back seat.

The cops managed to book him and place him in a holding cell. The man was lethargic during this process, presumably exhausted from his long night. But Bell didn't take any chances and shoved the prisoner into the cell with his hands still cuffed behind his back.

"Bell, you know the rules, no cuffs inside the cell," said Sergeant Weekly.

When the prisoner bent over and put his hands through the server hole, Bell reluctantly uncuffed him. Bell and Weekly walked halfway down the hall when they heard an enormous explosion.

"I thought a plane had hit the building," Bell said later.

In fact the prisoner – 5"9', 150 lbs. – had ripped the one-piece porcelain sink and toilet out of the wall and thrown it against the cell bars, where it shattered into a million pieces.

After they recovered from the shock, Weekly told the rookie cop, "Get back in there and cuff the prisoner!"

Bell told me it was the only time in his career that he disobeyed a direct order.

--Harold Schroeder

I will close with this stray document I found in my father's treasure trove.

It was written many years after his resignation from the CIA. I'm sure of that because of the computer graphics.

Where this piece fits into the jigsaw puzzle I can't tell you. To me it looks like a page from a textbook on espionage. But my dad would never have attempted such a high-falutin thing.

I do love it though.

The Circle of Deception

This is my attempt to simplify, in a geometric way, the central conflict that hobbles the Agency's intramural cooperation: CI Staff and CIA Ops judge the value of defectors and their offerings in ways that are inversely proportional.

CI Staff looks a gift horse in the mouth. Their operational philosophy is: The greater the truth, the bigger the lie.

CIA Ops, on the other hand, examines the intel first and concludes: The more glittering the gold, the more valuable the source.

The reason the Agency continually struggles to resolve this conflict is that the CIA has no assets deep within the KGB; no mole in place inside the Lubyanka who can tell us who and what is real, and who and what is phony. We're flying blind.

And, in the words of pilots and co-pilots the world over, "When you're flying blind, everyone's entitled to their own opinion."

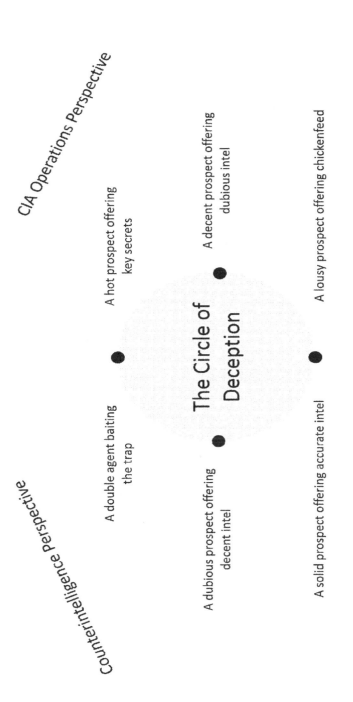

CIA Operations Perspective

Counterintelligence Perspective

The Circle of Deception

A hot prospect offering key secrets

A decent prospect offering dubious intel

A lousy prospect offering chickenfeed

A double agent baiting the trap

A dubious prospect offering decent intel

A solid prospect offering accurate intel

johnknoerle.com